# LIES AND LUST IN THE TUDOR COURT

# LIES AND LUST IN THE TUDOR COURT

The Fifth Wife of Henry VIII

*Margaret Doner*

iUniverse, Inc.
New York Lincoln Shanghai

# Lies and Lust in the Tudor Court
## The Fifth Wife of Henry VIII

iUniverse, Inc.

For information address:
iUniverse, Inc.
2021 Pine Lake Road, Suite 100
Lincoln, NE 68512
www.iuniverse.com

ISBN: 0-595-31301-9

Printed in the United States of America

*I dedicate this book to Katheryn Howard. Had you been born in the 21<sup>st</sup> century, things would have turned out much differently. You may have been guilty of adolescent yearnings and irresponsibility—but would still retain your head. In my mind you were a "wild child" trying to find your way in the world at a time when women had little or no freedom to choose their own path. Your spirit and energy never found a proper channel. I do not consider you a harlot, a whore, a stupid queen—but a girl overcome by the greedy ambition of those around you. You paid a high price for your passionate nature.*

# Acknowledgments

Thanks so much to all the people who helped me in the writing of "Lies and Lust in the Tudor Court: The Fifth Wife of Henry VIII." My Tuesday writing group—Amy, Angela, Dru, Elaine, Jeanne-Marie, Karen and Liz you have shared the many ups and downs that go hand-in-hand with a writer's life. My sister, Kalia, has always had a kind and supportive word of encouragement for me. My friend, Michelle, believes in me even when I don't believe in myself. And, to my husband, Chris, a wonderful friend and life partner—I am so grateful.

# PREFACE

The cold February dampness seeped from the stone floor through the soles of Katheryn's bare feet as she gazed at the block of wood she had requested. Come morning it would support her neck.

Outside her window, on the Tower Green, was the scaffold where she would kneel. Weak, her mind fogged by fear, she wobbled above the chopping block. She thought of others whose heads had fallen by order of the King. Anne Boleyn. It had been a clean cut. Then there was the poor Countess, Margaret of Salisbury. Tales of her messy beheading stirred the air for days afterward. The executioner had been a novice, the axe dull, and it came down over and over, hacking at the neck and torso of the sixty-eight year old woman before she succumbed. Katheryn could not bear the same to happen to her. The shame of public suffering prompted her now to lower her small body toward the floor.

She was afraid to touch the worn wood. Then all this would be, at last, made real. She closed her eyes and willed herself to breathe. The exhalation sent her body forward until she could feel her tiny neck and shoulders upon the smooth surface of the block.

"Dear God," she said, "you have not prepared me for this. How do I do this? I do not know how to die. I do not know how to die!" Her cries echoed upon the stone walls.

She raised her torso, and on her knees, hands clasped together, she prayed to God for strength. She could not hear His voice.

Yes, she was a sinner—an adulteress whose treasonous actions against the King sealed this fate. Still she could not banish the tender memories of Thomas Culpeper from her mind. "He lives in my heart," she whispered. "And now I pay for the sin of my own heart. Cut it out! Cut it out! It is the offender, not my head. I have loved and I will be punished for it!"

She looked again at the chopping block, breathed in its aroma—the stench of bloody death—and noticed a streak of brown blood left by the previous user.

"I was Queen of England. Do I not deserve a fresh piece of wood upon which to lay my head? Damn him to Hell! I shall never forgive him. Henry you fat, puss-ridden, monster! I hope you burn in Hell for your crimes! Burn in Hell! Burn in Hell!"

She reached out her hand to the crucifix on the wall above her. "Forgive me. Forgive me, God. I do not mean to curse the King. I am the evil one. Do not be angry with me."

Weary and desolate, she collapsed on the floor. Had I not been his favorite? He loved me above all the others. I was his beloved. His 'rose without a thorn.'

Perhaps tomorrow…

# CHAPTER 1

Katheryn Howard's breasts pressed against Edward's chest, as her right finger silenced his lips.

"SSSHHH," she whispered close to his face.

"Katheryn!" A man's voice boomed across the courtyard.

"It's Henry Mannox," Katheryn said to Edward, the young stable-boy beneath her. "He is taken with me. Do not let him know we are here."

He nodded his head and widened his eyes. A wrinkle registered on his brow. "You needn't fear," Katheryn said. "He has no claim on me. He will do you no harm." Edward was not fully convinced. A simple romp among the hedges was all he wanted and he had no desire to enter into a scuffle on her behalf.

The crunching of the leaves next to the hidden couple signaled the arrival of Henry Mannox, but he did not look beneath the shrubbery, unaware of the lovers who were inches away from his feet. "Katheryn, it is time for your music lesson."

When he disappeared, Katheryn popped up and brushed the dirt from her dress. She reached a hand to help the slightly shaken Edward to his feet.

"That was wonderful, my dear friend," she said and stroked his cheek. "I must be off now. Henry Mannox awaits." Katheryn disappeared around the corner. "Here I am Master Mannox. I am ready for my lesson on the virginal."

In 1537, Horsham Estate in England was ruled by Agnes, Dowager Duchess of Norfolk, a testy old crone, who had been put in charge of raising Katheryn from the age of ten. The Duchess, a wealthy, influential woman, was Katheryn's grandmother. Although Katheryn was a Howard, a noble name with a noble lineage, her father, Lord Edmund Howard, was not a wealthy man. Careless decisions and a notable lack of intelligence in matters of politics had left him debt-ridden. With ten children to care for he had been more than happy to be relieved of some of his burden and so it was that Katheryn came to live with her grandmother and one hundred servants. It was an arrangement that made it quite easy for Katheryn to have her way.

Henry Mannox reached out his hand and surprised Katheryn with a forceful grab at her arm as she raced by him. "I beg of you, if indeed you feel as I do, show me some token of your love."

"What token shall I show you? I will never marry you. I am a Howard." She stood on tiptoe to bring their faces closer. "It would never be allowed. A Howard woman could never marry a mere music teacher."

Henry scrunched his tall, lean figure almost in half to breathe in the aroma of Katheryn's hair, then drew back to scan the surroundings for a glimpse of the Duchess or one of her spies. "An intimate moment is all I ask of you."

"Perhaps, Henry, I can grant you an intimacy. But certainly not here and now. Besides, it is time for my lesson. Have you forgotten?" She moved her body back and forth against his chest then released herself and walked away toward the house. "Come Henry. I am waiting." Helpless, Henry staggered after her as though he were a puppet drawn by a string fashioned by the words, "Perhaps, Henry…"

A cold, damp silence assaulted Henry when he pushed open the door to the Duchess' chapel. The candles cast lacy shadows upon the vaulted ceilings.

"Katheryn?" he whispered. He was certain she had not yet arrived. Her presence excited him and filled the air with a vibration he was convinced he would recognize even blindfolded. Alone, he seated himself on the steps of the altar to await her arrival. He closed his eyes and imagined her body weakening under his power. Tonight she is mine. Let tomorrow take care of itself.

He wondered which pleasures of the flesh Katheryn would deign to consider him worthy of. The cold seeped into his buttock and thighs and he stood and slapped himself on the legs to warm them. He turned to face the Madonna and Child and performed a quick cross silently asking them to turn their eyes away from the act he was about to commit. A rustle outside the chapel caused Henry to duck down behind the pew.

Katheryn breezed in and slammed the door behind her. "Henry?"

"SSSHH, you make too much noise." Henry rose to greet her. "Katheryn, I thought I would burst from the waiting."

"You worry too much, Henry. I am here as I said I would be."

Henry rushed forward and grabbed her with both arms.

"Slowly. There is no reason to hurry. I find my greatest pleasure in the moment when two sets of lips still question whether or not they shall meet."

Shamed, Henry retreated, but watched her movements as a cat might stalk a bird hopping to-and-fro across the lawn. To pounce too quickly would result in a startled disappearance. Timing was of the essence.

"Master Mannox, you appear quite handsome by candlelight. Which intimacy has your mind settled on?" She stared into his eyes and let her tongue slip from her full lips in wicked temptation.

"Oh, Katheryn!" Henry rushed at her, no longer able to concern himself with the finer details of lovemaking. He chewed on her neck and lifted her from the ground to a more private place behind the altarpiece. Katheryn giggled, amused by his ardor. "Are you afraid that the delicacies you so desire shall disappear from my body at any moment? I assure you, I own these treasures and they are mine for as long as God wills it." She had learned early on how to weaken a man.

"I know how to meddle with you," she whispered in his ear, "without fear of making a child." She unfastened his codpiece.

"Oh, Katheryn," Henry said again, as the door burst open and the Duchess' shrill voice announced her presence.

"Katheryn, wicked child, I know you are in here. Mr. Mannox, I know you are with her. Get up!"

Katheryn stepped aside while Henry scrambled to his feet. "Grandmother, which one of your spies informed you of my meeting with Mr. Mannox?"

"Evil child. Henry, you are even more to blame than the girl. Didn't I entrust you with her musical education and nothing more? Get out before I take a rod to both of you!"

Katheryn squeezed herself between the Duchess and the holy water font leaving Mr. Mannox to defend his actions.

# CHAPTER 2

❀

"I am moving the household," announced the Duchess to Katheryn some months later. "We are going on to Lambeth, which lies a few miles from London. I am pleased to inform you that Mr. Mannox will not accompany us." She had not witnessed any further wrongdoing between Katheryn and her music teacher, but was far from convinced they had put an end to the affair.

Katheryn showed no emotion as she sat and rubbed the Duchess' feet.

"Dear child. That feels entirely wonderful," said the old woman and closed her eyes so tightly that they seemed to disappear beneath the wrinkles of her deeply creased face.

Henry Mannox, unbeknownst to the Duchess, had a new position in the household of Lord Bayment, a location that put him within striking distance of the Norfolk House at Lambeth. Katheryn, aware of Henry's change in employment, was certain she could continue her affair with him should she desire to. "I am most excited about the move, grandmother dear."

Her agreeable reply surprised the old woman. "Your uncle, the Duke of Norfolk, will see to it that you arrive there safely. Now leave me alone. I am near collapse with the weight of my responsibilities."

Three days of rain made all the roads, even the main one through the town of Tyburn, almost impassable. The wheels of the creaky, wooden carriage became so encased in mud they threatened to stop altogether. With little else to look at, Katheryn stared at her uncle's face until she could stand it no longer. To pass the time she imagined him as different animals. Nothing cute and furry she thought, more like a mackerel or perhaps a rat.

She couldn't believe that her father and this man were brothers. Her mother died when she was young, and although it had been three years since she had seen her father, she remembered him as handsome in a gentle way. He had delicate thin fingers, receding ash-colored hair and watery ice blue eyes.

The last time she saw him he had come out from the house, tears on his cheeks, sat next to Katheryn, and laid his head in her lap. Katheryn's stepmother had beat on him for pissing the bed due to illness. "Father, what is the matter?" she had asked.

"If I were a poor man's son, I might dig and delve for a living. My noble pride keeps me in poverty and my respect for women enslaves me. If I perform manual labor to support my family I bring shame upon the house and if I raise my hand to the wife I bring shame upon myself," he told her.

She was aware that people talked poorly of him. During the War of the Roses the Howard's loyalty to the Yorkist crown almost destroyed them. But in 1513 when her grandfather distinguished himself at the battle of Flodden Field, Henry VIII restored his title and estate. Since then her uncle, the Duke of Norfolk, had made himself into a successful advisor to the King. Katheryn's father had not prospered.

"Dirty, wet mongrels," said the Duke as he looked out his window at the people of Tyburn.

The roads were so jammed with wretched bodies moving from shop to shop that Katheryn wondered if the carriage would get through even in dry weather. "Why are all these people in the street, don't they know the wet drizzle will kill them if it gets into their bones?"

She glanced from the window and stared into the black, muddy face of an urchin, who picked his ear with a chapped finger and then spat at her carriage in disdain. She jumped back into her seat, startled by this unprovoked display of anger.

Her uncle, furious the driver couldn't move the carriage any faster, sank into a black gloom and scowled at her. "Filth and carnage. I would be on horseback if it weren't for you."

No sooner had these words escaped his lips than the sound of a trumpet reached their ears. "What is that?" asked Katheryn.

"The King's soldiers. Maybe they will do away with this ignorant cuss of a driver," said her uncle. "Move the damn carriage!"

Slowly the carriage pulled its heavy wheels through the mud and off to the side. Katheryn's desire to see the soldiers caused her right hand to seize the door and thrust it open before her uncle could stop her. The call of the horns drew her onward. Her skirts dragged in the mud, but she lifted them out with both hands and pushed herself onward.

"Get out of my way," she said rudely to a young boy about her age, remembering the stream of spit that had been directed at her. He studied her clothing—it declared her in a class superior to his—then shoved his right shoulder and thigh hard into her and landed her on her bottom. Not to be outdone, Katheryn sprang to her feet and delivered a hard blow to his retreating back.

Pleased with her response, the boy sneered and leaned in close. "They're Catholic priests," he whispered, "traitors to the King."

Katheryn had no idea what he was talking about. He smiled to reveal blackened and chipped teeth and blew a stream of snot from his nose that landed inches from Katheryn's feet. "Loved God more than the King of England, is how my mother put it to me."

At that moment the soldiers appeared, proud and elegant; six of them riding grand horses, each adorned with the insignia of Henry VIII. "The King's men," said Katheryn, wanting to appear as knowledgeable as the boy. Just then she saw the bodies, and let out a gasp of horror. The boy laughed at her squeamishness. "I saw three of them hung last week," he said proudly. "Eyes popped from the head of one of them."

Dragged by horses and tied to wooden hurdles, the bodies of five naked men came into view. They were still alive, but their flesh was bruised and beaten. Three of them were long and lean, one round and flabby, soft like gelatin, the other a muscular man with black curly hair.

"My God, what sinners must they be to suffer so?" she asked.

"The King has no need of a reason. If the King wants to cut off your head," he said, "then your head will roll. If you repeat I said that, I'll cut off your tongue." He grabbed her arm to sink his sharp fingernails into it.

Horrified, she ran beside the hurdles. The eyes of the black-haired man settled upon hers. Her shoes slipped in the mud, her hands pushed at the human roadblocks, but her eyes never left his. Not until the gallows came into view did Katheryn allow her gaze to drift upward toward the nooses.

The beaten bodies were untied and pulled up the stairs. The fat one muttered, but Katheryn couldn't catch the words until he screamed, "Henry shall burn in hell for all eternity!" It sent a cold fire down the length of her spine.

She watched the dark-haired priest and felt her heart reach out to him. He suffered so nobly. His body was taut and shivered. "God have mercy on your soul," she said again and again. The noose closed about his neck and the necks of the others. The benches beneath them were kicked aside, but the Kingdom of Heaven did not welcome them. No. They did not die.

Simultaneously, they withered and wiggled like worms at the end of a line. Faces blue, lungs gasping, they prayed for release. The King, however, did not want an easy death for these humble men of the cloth. An example must be made of all criminals. They were no exception.

When the breath no longer entered their bodies, a sudden blow of the axe cut the ropes and they fell with a thud onto the wooden platform.

"By order of his Royal Majesty, Henry VIII, King of England, they are to be mutilated before death," said the executioner.

He raised his sword and thrust it downward one at a time into the bowels of the men. Then he gutted them and threw the insides into the audience before an axe landed upon them. Arms, legs, and finally heads were flung into the crowd. Sickened by the sight, Katheryn ran from the mutilation and directly into her uncle who had come in search of her.

He grabbed Katheryn's arm and shook her until she was limp and weeping. "You are as wicked as the Duchess said. This may be your first public hanging, but it won't be your last. God and King punish sinners as they deserve to be punished. Henry Tudor is both the ruler of England and of the Church; if any man say differently then he shall suffer the consequences." He gave her a final shake and dragged her through the mud and back to the waiting carriage.

Weary from the journey, Katheryn breathed a sigh of relief when they pulled up in front of Lambeth Hall. After they witnessed the horrible mutilation of the priests her uncle had one method of communication, to lecture her on any subject he deemed worthy of her attention; his favorite being his loyalty to King and Church and how any traitor to Henry VIII deserved exactly as those men had gotten.

"These are dangerous times, Katheryn, and any man who declares himself faithful to the Pope shall die a traitor's death. Yet beware of reform, lest you take it too far. In his heart the King is a Catholic, of that there is no doubt. Follow the teachings of the Catholic Church, but denounce the Pope, and you will not go wrong."

Katheryn was fearful enough of her uncle to hold her tongue, but her face registered her disapproval at his heartlessness. The torture of the priests had not affected him at all. Her father would never have been so uncaring. But, her father wasn't here and her uncle was. That was how it was and how it would remain.

Holding her tongue had caused large creases to form beside her mouth, and at the bridge of her nose a worry-line began to settle. Even her luxurious auburn hair, loosened during the long journey, did little to soften her unhappy features.

The carriage had barely stopped before Katheryn jumped from it like a hound on the scent of a hare. Grace, not manners, was Katheryn's forte and she raced toward the Duchess' Lambeth estate happy to be free. A tall man stood before the doorway; he stepped forward to block her entrance.

Katheryn noticed his deep blue eyes, and the wavy black curls that crowned his head as he removed his cap to bow. She flipped her hair, proud that she had the opportunity to flaunt her mane at him. "Excuse me, you are in my way," she said.

Before he could reply, the Duke came upon this little encounter and grabbed Katheryn's wrist.

"Derehem. Master Francis Derehem, Your Grace," said the stranger and bowed once again in the direction of the Duke.

"Sir, I care not a whit about your name nor your title. If you are indeed a gentleman, you will step aside," said the Duke as he yanked Katheryn away from Derehem's interested gaze.

Compared to Horsham, the Lambeth estate with its enormous halls and outbuildings overwhelmed Katheryn. Its majestic appearance confirmed Katheryn's sense of her grandmother's social status—a powerful matron of the Howard noble line and godmother to both Princess Mary and Elizabeth. From its elaborate gateway and paved courtyard, to the great hall into which she stepped, it spoke to her of luxuries unknown except in her fantasies. She shuffled her feet through the rushes that covered the floor and stirred up the scent of rosemary. Although a large fire burned at one end of the room, it did not eliminate the chill.

As soon as her uncle turned away from her, she escaped out the door that led into the gardens. The first thing Katheryn noticed was the number of people who had gone outside to warm themselves in the sunshine despite the cold air. How elegant they were. She knew that the Norfolk House at Lambeth lay directly across the Thames River from Westminster palace and the royal court, and she imagined that these handsome well-appointed men, and richly attired ladies, were visitors from the King's court.

The scent of rosewater, lavender and musk filled the air. The men's hair was groomed, chin length and smooth. Their clothes were colorful, with doublets made of silk brocade, and codpieces decorated with points of linen or silk ribbon. Some of the women's headdresses framed their faces with gold cloth. Katheryn's gaze rested upon a man whose yellow hose revealed his amply built legs. How far away the spitting urchin of Tyburn seemed to her.

Ashamed of her unkempt appearance she smoothed her hair and pulled at her bodice. Her new life at Lambeth would require her to act the part of a lady. She studied the gracious manner the women moved their faces and hands when they addressed the men.

"I think I shall like it here a great deal," she whispered.

"I am certain of that." A man's voice returned in her ear and Katheryn wheeled round to see Master Francis Derehem leaning over her.

"In what manner are you certain?"

"Well, as you are a Howard, Katheryn, I believe."

"You haven't wasted any time in discovering my identity. My grandmother disclosed it perhaps?"

"Perhaps." He smiled. "It seems she is quite interested in introducing you to men of rank. She mentioned something about a music teacher of yours."

Katheryn blushed and in an attempt to maintain a fragment of dignity, walked away from him. He was unperturbed that he had embarrassed a lady, and followed her. "Did I mention that I am one of those men? A man of birth and substance. You could do worse than me. However, unlike your Mr. Mannox, I care not a whit for the virginal."

"Master Derehem, as you can see, I am in need of freshening after my long journey. I cannot present myself in such a condition. I ask that you let me retire and we continue this conversation at a later time." She brushed by him and then paused. Had his gaze followed her? Indeed, it had.

Katheryn entered the dormitory that would accommodate her. It slept all the girls at Lambeth. Most of them were related in the manner of cousin: first, second, third or fourth. They were daughters of noble families who desired a better life for their offspring—a life in closer proximity to the King's inner circle. A father knew there was nothing better he could do for his daughter than to place her nearer to the King's court. Only then would she be assured of a good marriage to a man of high rank.

Alice Restwold welcomed her with an arm around the shoulder. "I am your bedmate," she said.

Katheryn noticed rows of beds, each curtained for privacy, but close enough together to allow any sounds to filter through the drapes.

"That is unless someone else has come to visit for the evening," Alice continued. "There is an understanding," she hesitated to place an emphasis on the word, "among the ladies, that bedmates shall be changed to accommodate the needs at any time."

Katheryn stared at her.

"I hope I haven't offended you," Alice said.

"Offended, no. Confused perhaps."

"It is well known to all who reside here—except it seems the Duchess herself—that male visitors are not unknown in the ladies dormitory." Alice leaned in to whisper the next part. "And I would advise you not to be the one to tell her."

Katheryn laughed. "It seems that my reputation has been made available to Master Derehem, but kept from you. My grandmother sent me here to separate me from my music teacher, Henry Mannox. Our affair did not please her one bit, and she hopes to end it by my residence here. She has even thrust Francis Derehem in my direction. If she knew of the goings-on right under her nose, I suspect she would not have been so quick to send me away from Horsham to Lambeth. I think I shall like it here just fine."

# CHAPTER 3

Francis Dereham, Edward Walgrave, and Belford Griswold gathered up the many edibles into their hands. Francis grabbed the mutton and licked the juice off his greasy fingers with great delight. Belford, partial to sweets, scooped up apples and grapes, while Edward made certain that plenty of wine would be available to whet the throats of the maidens they were set to visit. It was a few minutes after midnight, well past curfew in the women's dormitory.

An ornate wrought iron gate, located at one end of a long corridor, blocked their entrance. Francis pushed against it. It didn't budge.

"Damn!" he said. "Alice Restwold promised to unlock it for us at the stroke of midnight. Now I shall have to pick it."

"Wait," Belford said. "Perhaps Alice never arrived because the Duchess interrupted her plans. Maybe we had best leave and return at a later time."

"What's the matter, Belford?" asked Francis. "Have you lost your taste for your lady so that you are this easily discouraged?"

"If Belford has lost his nerve it is because his lover hasn't the attraction for him that Mary Barnes has for me. I am certainly not to be so easily deterred," said Edward. "Pick the lock, Francis. I'll hold the mutton while you attempt it."

Edward thrust his torch forward to better illuminate the well-worn lock. "Tonight," Francis said as he deftly pried open the clasp, "Katheryn shall know the full measure of my intentions."

The men groped their way along the dark passageway that led to the women. A mouse scurried across the floor in front of Francis, and he stopped and motioned the others to do likewise. "What was that?" he whispered.

"A mouse, Francis," Edward said. "Pick up the pace, or I shall push ahead of you."

Francis paused at the heavy door that separated them from their lovers. His ears strained for sounds from within and he knocked lightly upon the wood. Edward, fed up with his caution, marched inside. Moonlight streamed into the still room through the long narrow windows, and the bed curtains glowed in its reflection. The men hesitated, taken back by the silence. Neither a flame, nor a breath of life marked the presence of a living soul. Francis looked at Belford, who looked at Edward, who shrugged his shoulders in confusion.

"Alice?" whispered Francis as he walked on tiptoe up the middle aisle between the beds.

"Mary?" Edward said as he followed behind. Belford, a bit more unnerved than the others stayed near the door. "Mary? It is Edward. Have you forgotten that I would come tonight? Perhaps they are asleep," he added in Francis' ear.

"I don't like this one bit," Belford said.

Suddenly a yell that reminded Edward of the time an old (and now quite dead) friend met the sharp side of an axe, erupted from Francis' throat and he dropped the mutton. Belford, already wound tight, gasped from across the room and threw the fruit high into the air, before he raced out the door.

A squeal of laughter began at the floor and circulated, until the room was alive with giggles and shrieks of delight. Katheryn, her hands still clasped about the ankles of Francis Derehem, slid on her belly from beneath the bed and rolled at his feet.

"These, dear ladies," she said, "are the gentlemen who we look to for bravery and protection. It seems my tiny fingers are enough to frighten all of them into dropping our banquet. Thank goodness for us that Edward held onto the wine. Master Derehem, it seems, thinks we should eat from the floor like animals."

"You wicked girl. The darkness holds evil and treachery and you are leader of this band of gypsies," said Francis.

"Not so wicked as wise," replied Katheryn. "It is true I organized this little surprise, but I had no idea who I would catch in my trap. Should the Duchess decide to pay us all a visit it is you who would be deemed evil, not I."

She reached out, grabbed some mutton, smiled at him and popped a large piece into her mouth. "Perhaps I have caught the biggest fish in the pond."

"Big enough that you shall feel fully satisfied, I can assure you," Francis said. He knelt down beside her to snatch the mutton away. "Katheryn does not wish to share my offering with the rest of you."

"It seems Master Derehem that you have met your match in Miss Howard," said Alice.

"We shall soon see. Edward, go and fetch Belford. He is probably cowering outside the door like a beaten dog."

Belford was indeed outside the door and Edward brought him into the dormitory.

"Come, Belford," Katheryn said. "I shan't hurt you. Your ankles need not fear the sting of my grim hands."

This sent another squeal of laughter about the room. Belford managed a small laugh and fell to his knees to retrieve whatever fruit he could find.

Francis took Katheryn's hand. "Spread out the cloth upon the bed. We shall eat the meat that is untouched, and drink the wine and see where this will lead us."

"Lead us?" said Katheryn. "Whatever do you mean? It seems to me that the presumption of your appeal to me is nothing but vanity. If your lips hold any promise of ever meeting mine they will be still so that mystery may hide any flaws."

Mary Barnes, eager to be alone with Edward, grabbed his hand, while Belford shyly offered Alice Restwold an apple. The bed curtains were drawn about Mary and Edward, but the others could hear the rustling of bodies upon the straw mattress.

"Tell me, Master Derehem, is this something you yourself have experienced?" Katheryn asked as she glanced toward the curtained bed.

"My tongue, upon your request, is silenced." He lifted the jug of wine and drank before he passed it to Katheryn.

"Close your eyes," she said. Francis obeyed eagerly.

Katheryn tore off a small piece of meat and placed it to his lips. "Open your mouth." She placed the mutton inside his mouth and manually closed his jaw. Francis opened his eyes and stared directly into hers.

"Tell me, did the Duchess put you up to this?" said Katheryn. "Is marrying you her intention for me?"

"The Duchess has her mind, and I have my own," Francis said. "I should not be so eager to oblige the Duchess if my own heart and eyes were not moved by the very nature of her request."

"You seem to think my heart and mind are equally moved. My music teacher has laid claim to me."

"A Howard marry a lowly music teacher? You shall have to produce a worthier suitor to make me jealous. Henry Mannox has no claim upon you, and I suspect that even if he did, you would not be so eager to honor it tonight."

Katheryn reached out to slap him, but he was too quick for her and grabbed her wrist. "Let me go!"

"Now you shall have a bit of your own medicine," he said and grabbed hold of the other wrist and pulled her closer. Their faces were inches apart. Katheryn could feel his hot breath. Slowly, she leaned into him and brushed her lips against his cheek and blew a small wisp of air into his ear. The grip around her wrists loosened. Katheryn's tongue darted from her mouth and quickly wet his earlobe before retracting—Francis let go of her.

Freedom sent her to her feet, and nimble and light she raced from him to the other side of the bed. "I am quick," she said.

"But I am quicker," he replied and stood up to begin a chase, which easily ended with Katheryn backed up against the wall.

"Your intentions are marriage?"

"Indeed," he said, and placed his lips full upon hers.

# CHAPTER 4

"They hang together by their bellies as if they were two lovebirds!" Henry Mannox complained to his cousin Edward Walgrave. They stood in the doorway and gazed out upon the gardens to watch Katheryn and Francis embrace.

Henry's steel-blue eyes fixed upon Katheryn. "Her loveliness," he whispered. His hand followed the form of her body. "How the curves of her bodice..."

"It seems Katheryn is no longer interested in your advances, dear cousin. I have seen with my own two eyes the kisses between Francis and Katheryn, and I can tell you they lie together as married nightly."

"This is unpardonable! The Duchess must stop these goings-on." Henry stamped his feet, and waved his fisted hands in the air.

"Be careful what you say. For if the Duchess hears of it you shall spoil my own pleasure with Mary Barnes as well. I will find it hard to forgive you for that. Turn your eyes to another and forget about your Katheryn," said Edward.

The color rose in Henry's cheeks and his clenched fists trembled. "I will kill him for the dishonor he does."

"A lady can hardly be dishonored if she enjoys and encourages the advances of the gentleman," Edward said.

They both stared at the lovers, who it seemed, could barely contain themselves from ripping off Katheryn's green and gold bodice. Her body pressed into Francis' and her hands slipped down his thighs.

"It is certainly apparent that no force is required on Francis' part." Edward laughed.

Henry grabbed Edward's shoulder. "Take it back! I won't hear you speak of her that way."

"I think perhaps you need to find yourself a lovebird to press against your own belly, and soon, or you shall regret your actions" said Edward and walked away, with a shake of his head.

Henry stumbled down the stairs and into the gardens. Dazed, eyes fogged by jealousy, he drew closer to the couple until he stood with merely the apple tree between them.

"Husband," whispered Katheryn. "I place everything I am into your eager hands."

Henry wrapped his arms tightly about his waist and felt his temples pulse with anger.

"Katheryn, to love a wife is luxury indeed. If pleasure is love, and I believe it to be, then I have known love abundant since falling into your arms," Francis said.

Henry could stand no more and stepped from behind the tree to confront them. "Wife? How dare you call her wife when she is no such thing. I demand an explanation."

Francis and Katheryn jumped apart, frightened by the intrusion. "Henry," said Katheryn. "What are you doing? Where have you come from?"

Francis quickly regained his composure and responded with a sharp blow to Henry's chest. "If you know what is good for you, you will leave and never return. I shall call Mistress Howard wife, and be called husband by her, and you have nothing to say about it. She has no use for you. If you bother us again I will consider it a challenge and your life will be worth no more than the ground upon which you stand."

"Katheryn?" Henry's eyes implored her to love him.

"Please, Henry, you must leave now," she said and turned away.

Henry scowled at Francis. "You haven't heard the last of me," he said as he stomped off into the estate.

Sunday, damp and dreary, found the Duchess, joints aching, moving slowly toward the chapel. "The rushes need changing," she said to her gentlewoman. "See to it that it is done immediately. Freshened with rosemary and lavender. Sunday or not, I want the floor fresh by nightfall."

"Yes, Your Grace," said the young girl who helped the Duchess along with an arm at her elbow.

The chapel door opened ahead of her and the Duchess saw Henry Mannox hurry out and down the hallway. "I know a few sins he would do well to ask for absolution of. He had best turn around if he knows what's good for his soul."

No sooner had those words left her mouth than Katheryn breezed up behind her.

"Morning, Your Grace." She smiled sweetly and rushed past the old woman.

"Katheryn! What in devil's name was Master Mannox's reason for his brief visit to our chapel this morning? I won't have him sully my altar again!"

Katheryn stopped abruptly, her hand on the door. "Are you certain it was Henry Mannox? Perhaps you are mistaken."

"Mistaken? Don't try and fool me with your innocent smile. I've got my eye on you," the Duchess said and rapped her with the walking stick.

Katheryn hurried into the chapel to avoid another hit from the old woman's cane and glanced to her left. Placed upon the seat reserved for the Duchess of Norfolk, was a sealed letter. She stepped into the pew to steal a peek at the seal. "It's from Henry Mannox," she whispered.

"What's that? A letter? Hand it to me."

"Yes, Your Grace." Katheryn hesitated. Then she presented the letter to the old lady.

"Now sit down. We shall discuss this later." She settled her body, upright and righteous, onto the hard wooden pew.

Katheryn sat down as instructed but could not concentrate on the service. The letter, she was certain, held nothing but bad news for her and Francis. Thankfully, it was still unopened. Katheryn fidgeted her foot back and forth and lifted and dropped her hands into her lap. Perhaps if she could get the Duchess' attention away from the note she would forget about it. Then she could snatch it up and hide it.

As if she had read her mind, the Duchess picked up the letter and placed it in her lap. She folded both hands securely atop it. Katheryn would soon hear of her displeasure.

Katheryn's face soured and she lowered her eyes. I'm doomed, she thought.

"Katheryn!" screamed the Duchess, her face twisted in rage, when she confronted her later that day. She waved the letter from Mr. Mannox at her. "What is the meaning of this?"

"I can't possibly say until I know the contents." Katheryn backed up closer to the door. Her eyes scanned the Duchess' bedroom for protection. A raised bed curtained with red and gold brocade fabric, stood before her. A small chair and chamber pot were placed near it. Before the roaring fire sat a wooden tub—obviously the lady was planning a much infrequent bath.

Where was the maidservant? She must have sent her away. Perhaps she wished no witness to her actions. She means to harm me for certain. She noticed a small basin near the tub and inched her way toward it. Should it become necessary, she planned to lift it and deliver a single blow to the old woman's skull rather than suffer repeated blows to her own head from the hard cane.

"Show the letter to me and I will better defend myself," Katheryn said. She longed to know the exact contents.

"Never mind," said the Duchess and turned to place the letter in a coffer. "Master Mannox has proven himself friend to me, although I suspect his intentions were merely to be a foe to Master Derehem. He informs me of nightly goings-on, not only between you and Francis Derehem, but between other ladies and their lovers as well. What do you say in your defense?"

"Defense? Francis Derehem spoke of marriage and calls me wife. A wife and husband must defend a display of affection between them? This is something new, Your Grace."

"Wife?" said the astonished Duchess. "Husband?"

"The law makes husband and wife of two consenting adults, who have known each other repeatedly, does it not?"

"You dare to stand there and inform me who shall be your husband? That you would make such an arrangement is unthinkable! Have you forgotten you are a Howard and noble by birth? If your immoral body ruled such a decision I dare say that more than half of Lambeth would call you wife today."

This accusation enraged Katheryn and she placed her hands upon the basin, ready not to split the old woman's skull, but to send the basin crashing, in defiance, to the floor. A knock on the door stilled her hands on the rim of the bowl.

"What?" said the Duchess.

"It is me, Your Grace. Come for your bathing," said the meek servant as she inched her way into the room.

The old lady sat herself in the hard wooden chair. The exchange with Katheryn had worn her out and, suddenly feeling her age, she was glad for the opportunity to momentarily forget the contents of the letter and the words just spoken. She had done her duty and now she wanted Katheryn gone and the quiet of her room restored. She closed her eyes and leaned backward.

"Be gone with you." She wagged her finger toward the door.

Katheryn wanted nothing more than to be out of there. However, the contents of the letter still intrigued her. She moved closer to her grandmother. Her gaze rested on the open coffer. The servant had begun to undress the old lady. On tiptoe, Katheryn walked behind them, grabbed the letter and ran from the room with it clutched to her bosom.

"I shall kill him with my bare hands!" yelled Francis. "My sword is too good for the body of that black beast." Although not large, Francis with his chest puffed in anger and his sleeves puffed, as was the style, was almost doubled in size. Katheryn admired the manner he strutted his body before her. When he planted his legs firmly to the ground, she was certain she could spend her life with him; for never, she thought, had she known a more proud and elegant man.

"Oh, most noble gentleman, dear Francis, run him off, let him feel the sting of your fist, but spare his life. He cannot help himself, for it is his overwhelming passion for me that leads him to behave this way," Katheryn said. "I dare say that you must find it hard to blame poor Henry. After all, the feelings that I arouse in you might cause similar behavior if the tables were indeed turned."

Francis walked to Katheryn and gently laid his hand upon her tiny shoulder. Her large green eyes, flecked with gold, implored him to soften. What is it about this woman he thought? Her diminutive stature made him long to protect and care for her, and the fire that burned within her, inflamed him.

"He is no real threat to me," he said. Behind his statement, however, seemed to linger the hint of a question.

"None," she whispered and drew a finger across his lips.

"Then I shall punish him with fists alone and demand he be gone for good, if that is to your liking."

"I no longer care for him, but I should like to see him remain alive. Send him away so that we might love without interference."

# CHAPTER 5

Katheryn wiped a crust of sleep from the corner of her eye and shifted her body on the straw mattress. Alice Restwold, her back pressed against Katheryn's, mumbled to herself and dug a heel into her bedmate's calf. Katheryn thrust back and pushed Alice closer to the edge of the bed. Annoyed, Alice twisted around, flopped onto her back, and then tossed her arm over Katheryn's head.

"Alice!" Katheryn said. "You are a horrible bedmate. You squirm and turn all night and talk in your sleep. I long for Francis next to me. These weeks with him away have been unbearable."

"You are worse than me," Alice said. "You swivel and shift—you call out, 'Francis.' If you climb on top of me, I shall scream and throw you to the floor."

Katheryn gave Alice a last jab to the ribs, rose from her bed, walked to the window and threw it open. It was the first time she felt the breath of spring. The birds chirped in the trees, the sun poked through the clouds, and Katheryn inhaled deeply and shook her head and stretched. The newly warmed air and the promise of a peaceful day lifted her spirits enough to send her back to the bed in apology.

"I'm sorry, Alice," said Katheryn. "Let's do forgive one another." She held out her hand and Alice squeezed it. "I shall be as happy as you for Francis' return."

Katheryn glanced toward the window. Something caught her eye, and she leaned out to witness the approach of six men on horseback. Her uncle, the Duke, was one of them. "He's back. I will do my best to avoid an encounter with him."

She dipped her hands into a basin of water on the nightstand, and splashed a bit on her chest and throat. Even from the window she could see a scowl on the Duke's face as he dismounted and handed the reins to a stable-boy. *He looks ridiculous. He thinks he's King of England the way he struts.*

She fastened her bodice about her and lifted her thick hair from her neck. "Alice? Shall we take a walk through the gardens today? I must be certain to stay out of the path of my uncle. Will you join me?"

"I'd love to," Alice said.

Katheryn nodded and slipped her feet into the tiny, brocade shoes she had flung carelessly to the floor the night before. No sooner had she smoothed her skirts then the door opened. The Duchess appeared and smiled a broken and sinister grin. It was very rare for the Duchess to come to this room and Katheryn knew it must be extremely important for her to manage the steps necessary to reach the dormitory.

Alice gave her a stiff curtsey. "Your Grace," she said. Katheryn performed the smallest curtsey she thought she could get away with. All the girls present felt their hearts beat harder in their chest, and the same thought pierced each and every brain: *The Duchess is here to dole out punishment for our nightly romps with the men.* A whispered, collective, "Your Grace," circled the room.

"Katheryn, your uncle is here to present you with special and welcome news," the Duchess began with a clearing of her throat. "I should let him deliver it himself." She paused. She thought she would burst if she didn't tell Katheryn the reason for his visit. She reached out and grabbed Katheryn's arm and pulled her closer. Katheryn could feel the old woman's stale breath on her cheek. She turned her face away to avoid the stench, but the Duchess saw it as a sign to whisper her news into Katheryn's waiting ear.

"An appointment at court, as maid to the new Queen. Our King has selected a German princess for his fourth wife. A large, uncultured woman, they say. He made the decision from a painting of her and rumor has it that he regrets it already."

Katheryn's face showed her disbelief.

"But, that is no concern of yours," continued the Duchess, "Anne of Cleves is required to appoint English girls to serve her. You, my dear child, have been selected to serve the Queen in her inner chamber. Now run and don't let the Duke know I already told you his important message."

Eager to send Katheryn on her way, the old woman shoved her toward the door. "Now go see him. He waits for you in the Great Hall."

Normally the action of shoving Katheryn prompted a reaction, but she was so stunned that she merely stumbled toward the door and down the steps to meet her uncle. Impatient, as usual, he paced back and forth. A large leather purse swung from his hand. Occasionally, he whacked it with a loud thud against the stone fireplace. By the sound of the thud, Katheryn guessed there were a large number of coins housed inside the pouch. She also knew that if she angered him he might choose to hit her with it and she would feel the sting for many days. She entered the room deferentially, hoping to avoid such an action.

"Your Grace," she said sweetly and curtsied low.

"Katheryn." He greeted her with a hug and wrapped his left arm about her shoulders. "I am pleased to bring you this news. I arranged an appointment for you at Court. To the Queen of England. A maid-in-waiting to Anne of Cleves. Your cousin Mary Norris has also been appointed, and with these positions the Howards indeed move closer to the inner circle and have an even greater opportunity to make their influence felt. The King has always had a weakness for women with Howard blood. Has he not already taken one for a wife?" The Duke smiled down at Katheryn who kept her gaze upon the floor.

It was fortuitous thing for Katheryn that he could not read her mind. A good place for a girl to be if she wants to lose her head. If she were alive you could ask my cousin Anne Boleyn about the King's fondness for Howard women. Katheryn had heard stories of Anne Boleyn since childhood. How beautiful Anne was, how well educated, and intelligent. But she had also heard how evil an adulteress Anne was, and how fortunate she had been to receive the sharp edge of a sword, instead of the dull end of an axe. Katheryn's sympathies always lay with Anne, and she had never forgiven her uncle for sitting on the Council responsible for condemning Anne to death.

"A great honor indeed. A great day for me, and of course, for you." He swung the pouch of money back and forth in front of Katheryn's nose. "This is yours. Do not ask me why. Merely ask how you might earn such a reward. Do your job well and serve not only Her Majesty but your family's interests and you will have earned this."

Katheryn was speechless.

"What's the matter with you girl? Don't tell me you are a fool like your father. Don't you know what this means?"

"I am overwhelmed, Your Grace." Katheryn reached out her hands and the Duke filled her small palms with the weighty bag. It took both of her arms to hold it, and she smiled up at him. "This bodes well for me, dear uncle. I think perhaps I could become accustomed to a life at court."

"Of course you will. One idiot in the family is enough, and your father filled that role long ago. If he can't bring respect to the name of Howard, then you will. An honor such as this can not be refused. We leave in three days time. I will see to it that you arrive safely at the barge that will take you across the Thames. Now be gone, I've much to do."

Katheryn bowed and rushed from the room eager to share her good fortune with Alice.

"What does this mean for Francis?" Alice asked upon hearing the news.

"He is away. Who knows when he shall return?" said Katheryn.

"He plans to marry you."

"Alice, do you honestly think my uncle would allow such a union? Especially now?" She held up the purse.

"It is obvious that he has great plans for me."

"Francis won't like it."

"Tell me then, Alice, what am I to do? This is what my father hoped for me when he sent me to live with my grandmother. Shall I break his heart and defy my uncle as well? If I refuse this appointment I will shame the name of Howard. Besides, there isn't a woman in England who wouldn't kill for such a position."

"Granted, but that will matter little to Francis if it means losing you."

"Perhaps. Perhaps not. When he is away for many weeks do you honestly think he is faithful to me? Then you do not know men. It has been my experience that men are faithful to a woman as long as she is within arms reach. And besides, if Francis does truly mean to marry me, my good fortune may well be his in time."

"I thought you loved him."

"I do love Francis, but not so much that I am willing to risk the anger of my uncle and shame my father."

It was overcast on the day Katheryn left for court. A large black cloud formed above her. She stood onshore and studied it to determine its direction. She didn't relish the thought of crossing the Thames in the midst of a raging storm. The wind whipped at her cloak and pushed the hood from her head.

"Modesty is not your virtue," the Duchess told her this morning, "but you had best learn how to pretend you are well versed in the ways of a lady if you wish to please your Queen. Your hair shall be covered, your eyes shall be cast downward, and your single purpose shall be to serve." It seemed to Katheryn the Duchess got great pleasure in the idea of her serving *anyone* obediently, Queen or not.

Her uncle argued with the bargemen who felt it would be best to delay their journey until the storm had passed. The Duke wanted to leave immediately. Katheryn glanced at the cloud—then her gaze caught the figure of a man. "Derehem."

He pulled the horse around so that it stopped two feet from Katheryn and dismounted. "I've come back to the news of your departure! The Duchess informed me of your appointment. Thank God I caught you. You mustn't go. You were to be my wife." He grabbed her hands.

The Duke of Norfolk stopped his argument with the bargeman mid-sentence. "Unhand her! She is not yours to detain. She belongs to the royal court now."

"She called me husband," said Francis. She is mine!" He grabbed her hand and pulled her toward him.

"Katheryn is a Howard. She belongs first to her family, and it is in the best interest of her family that she serves the Queen. You must be insane if you think I would ever let her marry the likes of you! Waste such a treasure on a lowly man as yourself? Katheryn is destined for marriage to a man of much higher rank than Gentleman." He grabbed her arm.

Katheryn gazed first at Francis and then at her uncle. She knew who would win this battle, for no one, save the King, could make her uncle change his mind. The wind whipped her face, her eyes filled with tears.

"I won't forget you," Francis said, and released her.

"Oh yes, dear Francis," said Katheryn. She wiped her eye with the back of her hand and waved farewell as her uncle pulled her into the barge. Large raindrops beat down upon Francis as the boat pulled away from the shore.

# CHAPTER 6

✿

Katheryn arrived at Westminster and quickly realized that her life at Horsham and Lambeth had not adequately prepared her for a position in the King's court.

The Duchess' homes paled in comparison to her new extravagant surroundings. Above her now were bright green, yellow and gold ceilings, embellished with emblems and ornamental designs. Upon the walls hung tapestries rich in colored silk and decorated with precious stones. The courtier's colorful clothing was studded with jewels and the scent of the spice balls hanging from their bodies permeated the air with exotic aromas.

The number of servants far surpassed those of Lambeth palace. From the scullery boys who climbed inside the large iron pots to wipe them clean, to the highborn attendants of the privy chamber, Katheryn was immersed in the quickened pace of court life. Immediately her instincts told her that the rules were unspoken but rigid, and conforming to those that must be obeyed and those that could be broken would determine her success or failure as a courtier. She had to keep her senses keenly tuned and notice the spoken and unspoken messages that were being broadcast at a furious pace.

Unfortunately for Katheryn, all of the women of court felt rudderless. They looked to the Queen for direction, and Anne of Cleves was lost and alone. Her servants, who had come from her homeland to accompany her, had been sent back and replaced with English girls; the daughters and wives of men in favor with the King.

The new Queen's English was broken and heavily accented. She knew nothing of music, art and even her needlepoint was crude. But she smiled kindly and nodded her head, almost as if she had been summoned to the court to serve them.

"You have music?" she asked Katheryn one day.

"Music?" Katheryn said.

"You know. To play. Make music." Anne walked over to the virginal.

"Oh, yes, Your Majesty. I can play."

"Please." Anne gestured to the instrument.

Katheryn took her place and paused. She wished she had devoted herself to her studies with Henry Mannox a bit more now. She looked around at her cousin, Mary Norris, who nodded in encouragement. She sat down and closed her eyes. She remembered a simple tune and let the music enter her body before playing a note. First her torso swayed side-to-side, and then she placed her hands upon the keys.

Slowly, then with greater confidence, she let the music flow from her body unto the keyboard. She had forgotten the words to the song, and also the title, but she remembered the melody and hummed along. Her voice was lilting and clear. Soon the others gathered about her and began to hum as well.

"I know the song you are playing," said Mary Norris. "It is *The Last Song for My Lady* I believe.

"Your Majesty, let me show you how to play it," Katheryn said suddenly and sprang up from her seat and gestured for Anne to take her place.

"Oh, no," Anne said and blushed.

"Please, Your Majesty, let me show you how." Katheryn stood beside her and placed her fingers upon the keyboard.

"Put your hands on top of mine." Anne gave her a look of confusion. "Mary, show her what I mean."

Mary lifted the Queen's hands and placed them on Katheryn's. Anne's rough fingertips scratched Katheryn's smooth skin and her ruddy coloring contrasted sharply with the whiteness of Katheryn's complexion. Katheryn played the notes one by one and the Queen followed. Her hands slipped from Katheryn's and she let out a giggle as her index finger hit a wrong note.

"It is good." She laughed. "Now I can entertain the King."

"Not yet!" Katheryn said. "You should wait a bit before attempting to make the King happy with your music."

"I wish to make the King happy," Anne said. She pulled her hands from Katheryn's and swung her body around to face the ladies. "I know I cannot."

"Oh, Your Majesty…" said Mary Norris breaking an awkward silence.

Anne lifted her hand to quiet her. "Please," she said and lowered her eyes as though Mary was Queen and she was the servant. "My friends call me Anna."

"But, Your Majesty…"

Anna lifted her hand once more. "Anna. No more words. We will play." She dropped her fingers onto the keys with a crash and turned toward Katheryn and smiled. "Now, Katheryn, we will play."

"Yes, Anna," said Katheryn.

Two weeks of early spring rain had left the ground muddy and the brown earth broke up under Katheryn's dainty feet as she led the Queen to her seat to view the first tournament of the season. Although a runner of fine red cloth spanned the length of the jousting field and the Queen managed to stay upon it, it was Katheryn's duty to lift Anna's skirts and this placed her in the muck. The tournament had not yet begun and already Katheryn's ankles felt the cold, wet earth around them.

She helped the Queen to her seat as the spring sun poked through the clouds, providing some relief to her icy fingers. She smoothed Anna's skirts and glanced across the field toward the King's entourage. Although over-weight, ill and unable to participate himself, Henry VIII enjoyed remaining close to the action and wandered about encouraging the champions, and arousing the anger of those less favored.

Katheryn studied Anna's face hoping to catch the slightest indication of her feelings. Rumors had been circulating of Henry's displeasure with this arranged marriage and his desire to be rid of her. Some said he used the words, 'Flanders Mare' to describe her and not once had he been able to do his hus-bandly duty and plant the seed. Anna's eyes followed the King closely, but her face registered no emotion.

She reminded Katheryn of a tortoise; well-armored, patient, thoughtful. Her head turned slowly, scanning the world around her, while occasionally she blinked her heavy-lidded eyes. When confronted, Anna withdrew inside her shell, and no amount of cajoling could bring her out until she was ready. Although only a few years older than Katheryn, she seemed ancient to her—yet extremely naïve. As far as Katheryn could tell, Anna had no idea that merely receiving a goodnight kiss from Henry wouldn't impregnate her. Katheryn had thought many times of informing the Queen that there was something more required of the King to conceive a child—and it was something Henry hadn't the will to do with her.

Both the King and Thomas Culpeper, a Groom of the Privy Chamber, were staring in the Queen's direction. But it wasn't Anna they saw. She did little to inflame the passion of these men; rather it was her lady-in-waiting who caught their attention. Even from a distance she awoke the predator in them.

Katheryn saw Culpeper. The male animal in its perfected form, he was graceful yet strong. She was certain Thomas Culpeper got the women he wanted. Katheryn noticed every gesture, every minute indication that he was aware of her. He erased all memories of Francis Dereham and matched the dangerous intensity she felt ever since she arrived at Court.

Because Anna preferred to sit in silence, Katheryn had time to watch the King and Thomas move toward them. She turned her body and fussed over the Queen's skirts, all the while aware of Thomas' approach.

She wished her dress was not so drab and looked enviously at Anna's new garment and the elaborate pearl and ruby cross around her neck. Wasted on her. She crossed her arms under her bosoms to lift them upward and catch Thomas' eye. The King stared at her.

It had never occurred to Katheryn, before this moment, that perhaps someone was receiving her signals other than Master Culpeper. Thomas glanced into Katheryn's eyes which registered fear in his direction.

"My Lord," Thomas said, interrupting the King's salacious reverie. "It is time for the games to begin." He gestured toward the field and placed an arm at the King's elbow. "Let me help you to your seat." He turned his head and smiled at Katheryn, who breathed a sigh of relief and gratefully returned the smile. Queen Anna raised her eyebrows, giving Katheryn little indication of her feelings.

The young Henry had been a handsome, healthy, vigorous man. His appetite for hunting, gaming, and women, needed to be satisfied constantly and earned for him a reputation much admired in a King. But this was neither the Henry to whom Anna of Cleves was wed, nor the man, who nearing fifty, eyed eighteen-year-old Katheryn with prurient intent. Riding accidents, rich foods and a quick temper had turned the admirable prince into an angry, pain-ridden, old monarch—certainly not qualities Katheryn found attractive.

"His Majesty appears more contented," Anna said to Katheryn in her typically calm manner.

Anna's English had improved with the aid of numerous tutors and Katheryn had come to believe that there was a quick mind behind the Queen's stoic façade.

"Yes, Your Majesty."

The next day, Thomas Cromwell, the Lord Privy Seal, detained Katheryn in the hallway.

"Mistress Howard." He hurried toward her.

"Yes, My Lord." They had never been formally introduced.

"Lord Cromwell."

"Yes, My Lord, I know well who you are." She couldn't imagine why he had detained her.

He gave her a slight tug on the arm to indicate he wished her to come in closer. "It's a private matter."

Katheryn nodded. "Yes? Private? Concerning what?"

"The King."

Katheryn raised her eyebrows. "The King, My Lord, what could the King possibility want with me? Perhaps you are mistaken."

"No mistake. He wishes to see you alone this afternoon. I will escort you myself at three o'clock."

He disappeared down the hall, and didn't look back at her.

It was Cromwell who arranged the marriage to Anna of Cleves. In a desperate last attempt to earn the King's good graces Katheryn feared that Cromwell had decided a mistress would help the King forget his sexual dissatisfaction with the Queen.

"The King is happier with me?" Anna touched Katheryn's shoulder.

"I'm certain he is, Anna. Your English has improved." It embarrassed Katheryn that the Queen was so unguarded when she was around her. What was her role? To be the Queen's friend and call her Anna? To agree with her every statement? Or merely to serve her every whim?

She needed to be alone. Bowing to the Queen she asked to be relieved of her duties. Anna granted it.

Katheryn took refuge in the gardens to think. Everything was happening much too quickly. On the one hand it was King of England who had summoned her and she couldn't help but feel honored. On the other hand, she knew he could be a beast, who had no problem dismissing his wives with either the stroke of an axe or the signature of a pen.

She wandered among the hedges, then paused and plucked the tough, little evergreen leaves one-by-one from the thick bushes. Her fingers tore the greenery into small pieces that dropped to the ground at her feet. Her mind circled, dancing around her predicament but finding no solution. A crackle of twig startled her to attention and she twirled about to find the King of England a mere three feet from her.

"My Lord," she said, bent her knees, and wiped her fingers briskly together to clear them of the leaves sticky residue. She had never seen the King alone and she glanced around, certain that his nervous courtiers were hidden close by. She never considered that a King would stand for even a moment in time by himself, not surrounded by servants and confidants. His aloneness made him seem smaller to her, and softer. Less frightening. His smile was almost timid, and his tiny eyes were childish and shallow. Adorned in his finery he looked out of place among the simple garden shrubs and she clutched her hands at her waist nervously.

She smelled his breath: cold pork tinged with ale. In the daylight she noticed his face had small purple veins sprouting here and there, and his eyebrows were thin and arched in a state of perpetual questioning. His strong hands grasped at her upper arms and he lifted her from the ground and drew her toward him.

"Katheryn," he whispered. It frightened her that he should be so bold, and that alone with him she could do nothing to resist, nor was there anyone to disapprove of his public attentions.

"My Lord," she said breathlessly. His face came closer and his cheeks were now only inches from her own. His soft, formless lips pressed against hers and encased them without finding a home. Their rubbery texture prevented the hard, vibrant contact that she found so exciting in her other lovers. She squeezed her eyes tightly, hoping that the King would withdraw and allow her to breathe once again.

When the kiss was completed he gave her a look that she imagined he must give the game he had successfully cornered and was about to kill. His hands touched her white throat and stroked the flesh about her neck back and forth until small bumps appeared on it.

"I have aroused you," he said. "I shall be the first to awaken the woman in you, Katheryn. And you shall bear me a son."

He was so matter-of-fact, so certain of himself that Katheryn did not move, nor say a word. Henry ran his hands up and down her body as though claiming his territory at last. He paused at her breasts and winked as he lifted her skirts inches from the ground.

"I feel like a young man. You excite me, Katheryn," he said and pulled her body hard against his. He wrapped his fat arms around her until they encircled her completely, like a snake strangling its prey.

# CHAPTER 7

Thomas and Katheryn toyed with one another from a distance, growing ever more eager for contact as the night's festivities wore on. Thomas' softly upturned lips set off the down-turn of his eyes and together they radiated sensuality. His hair lay flat and smooth in perfect frame to his face. Something deep inside told Katheryn that he was not afraid of a woman; that he had studied the ways of pleasing the flesh and was eager to put it to the test on her body.

So strong was the seductive scent he broadcast that Katheryn never noticed the King watching her. Culpeper's attentions had momentarily erased Katheryn's concern that the King meant to have her for his own.

Henry and Anna sat side-by-side raised above the others, observing the revelers, enjoying the music and the merriment of the court jester. The court knew the King's real interest lay elsewhere.

"You haven't stopped dancing all night long, Katheryn. How will Master Culpeper lay his hands upon you if you don't stand still?" said Mary Norris.

Katheryn lifted her eyebrows and smiled. "You are suggesting that Thomas Culpeper has an interest in me? I hadn't noticed."

Mary laughed. "You dance by, swish your skirts, and fall into his eyes. He paces about the room like a tiger tethered to a pole and unable to leap upon its prey. If each of you is oblivious to the flirtations of the other then I'd say something is very wrong."

"I would know what to do with him if he laid his hands upon me," Katheryn said. "Would you?"

"If Thomas Culpeper had an interest in me I should think I had been blessed, but that will never happen. He's yours, Katheryn."

The color rose in Katheryn's cheeks. Her brown and red velvet gown trimmed in gold set off her hair and face as they shone in the candlelight. Thomas walked toward her and extended his hand. The lively Galliard, Katheryn's favorite dance, drew them onto the floor, but soon the Pavane slowed them down. His hand touched hers and his body drew close until Katheryn could feel its heat radiate onto her skin. The half smile on his lips never fluctuated as Thomas secretly slipped a note into Katheryn's open palm.

She was stunned. Her feet, moments before smooth and confidant, tangled in her skirt and sent her onto the floor with a crash. Thomas reached down and swept her up, "I adore you, Katheryn," he said, before releasing her and continuing the dance. All this happened so quickly, with such grace, that most never witnessed the event. One man, however, saw each and every nuance. Henry VIII did not like it at all.

The other observer was Mary Norris, and she signaled to Katheryn to drop from the dance and join her. Katheryn, flustered from her fall, curtsied and excused herself, but Thomas would not let her retire unattended and followed her to Mary's side. Katheryn's hand still clutched the note and Thomas' eyes glanced repeatedly toward it, as if to say, 'Read it.' Slowly she opened the crumpled message, careful to keep it close to her breast and hidden. As she read the words, he leaned in to speak them into her ear. Mary, unwilling to miss a moment of the courtship, stayed and wondered what sounds passed between them.

The color that rose in Katheryn's face told Mary that they were words of love and passion. But Katheryn and Thomas were not aware of Mary, for at that moment all others had disappeared. Katheryn whispered in Thomas' direction, "My love," before she placed her hand once again in his.

The room fell silent as the King rose up from his seat and signaled to the musicians. The dancer's feet stopped, the courtier's chatter ceased.

"The Queen wishes to retire for the evening," he announced. Immediately Katheryn and Mary rushed to her side to escort her from the room. Thomas returned to his place and stood stiffly beside the King. When Anna had gone, Henry looked over at Thomas, but Thomas stared straight ahead and did not acknowledge him. With a wave of his hand Henry motioned to the others to continue with the dancing and merriment, but still Thomas did not move.

"She is lovely," Henry said in Thomas' direction as the music once again filled the room.

"The Queen is very lovely, Your Majesty. You are a lucky man," replied Thomas.

"It is not the Queen about whom I speak."

"Your Majesty?" Thomas said politely.

"I notice Katheryn has caught your eye."

"Your Majesty?" he said again with just the right amount of inflection to remain neutral.

"The young Mistress Howard. You caused a flush to rise in her bosom this evening."

"The Galliard makes red the faces of all those who attempt it," Thomas said.

"What do you think of this arranged marriage I find myself in?" Henry asked suddenly.

"Your Majesty?" Thomas was genuinely stunned by the King's boldness.

"Come with me, Thomas." Henry rose from his seat and took Thomas' arm in his strong fingers. "Leave us," he commanded the others who had immediately come to attention to serve the King's next desire. "I wish to be alone with Culpeper."

Waves of bodies swept aside with a bow to allow them passage. Henry led Thomas out the door and into the hallway. Lingering courtiers and soldiers looked with terror at the arrival of the King, alone and unguarded. A wave of his hand sent them scurrying like mice down the corridors. Culpeper was frightened, but outwardly he remained calm and earnest, his full attention turned toward Henry.

"I like you, Culpeper. I do not like Anna. Her hanging breasts and the looseness of her flesh can not excite nor provoke any lust in me. I will never be steered to know her carnally. Cromwell will have to pay for his mistake. I like her not. I like her not at all."

Culpeper swallowed his next words. His thoughts raced. Cromwell? Thomas Cromwell had been the King's most trusted advisor for years. Thomas Cromwell was closer to the throne than anyone.

"Yes, Your Majesty."

"I must be rid of her. Cromwell has sickened me with his bad advice and political aims. I want the young Katheryn. In her I find the feelings I am denied in Anna."

"As mistress?"

"As wife. How will I bear another son if I cannot take my wife to bed? I will be frank with you, Culpeper. I must have another son. It is no secret that Edward is not strong. When I look upon Mistress Howard I find the fire still rages in my loins and I will not be denied. It is she who will bring an end to this barren reign."

Henry looked at Culpeper for signs of disappointment, but Culpeper did not work his way up in the ranks by being stupid and he showed Henry nothing of the feelings that tore at his insides. "Your Majesty, I am flattered that you share your most intimate thoughts with me. How may I serve you?"

"Must I state my mind aloud? Have I not two eyes to witness the night's activities? I took you for a smarter man than most." Henry glared at Thomas.

"No, Your Majesty. You make yourself perfectly clear."

"Good. I like you Culpeper. Let's return to the dances and enjoy the evening."

# CHAPTER 8

The afternoon sun cast long, dim shadows across the floor as Katheryn nervously awaited the arrival of her uncle, the Duke of Norfolk. Her stiff collar chafed her neck and she worked the fingers of her right hand down behind it, feeling itchy and raw in a line that extended from her throat to her breastbone.

Why had she been summoned and then left alone for so long? She walked absentmindedly to the window, but the thick lead glass blocked the view. She pushed at the latch to release it. Its stubbornness required both hands. When the Duke arrived at last, he found her struggling against the window.

"Ahem." He cleared his throat. She wheeled around and curtsied, a little off balance, in a gesture of insincere respect. His stare always reminded her of a fish. Sometimes she swore his pop-eyes moved separately as they scanned the room with razor-edged suspicion. The pasty flesh of his cheek gleamed coldly even in the heat.

She braced herself with her right hand on the nearest chair as a tremor arose in her chest.

"Officially," said the Duke, "this is not to be considered a formal proposal." He scanned her face for a glimmer of understanding on her part of what he was about to propose. Her expression remained frozen, so he rushed on. "The King has expressed some interest in milady. I am here not to extend with any formality an actual proposal of marriage, but to make note of your reaction to such an offer."

"Marriage? The King? He is married to Anna."

The Duke came closer to make certain she understood clearly the importance of his words, and the closer he came to her, the more Katheryn understood. She glanced at his face and circled the chair to escape him.

"But, uncle," she said, "with all due respect, have you forgotten Francis Derehem? I am, by word, betrothed to him." Suddenly her past association with Francis became very important to her—she hoped their relationship would be enough to convey a message of disinterest to the King without provoking his anger.

The Duke grabbed Katheryn's arm until she felt the sting of his sharp fingers. "I have hinted at an offer to make you Queen of England, you little fool. To bring both you and your entire family into a position of great power and you speak of Francis Derehem!" His voice ended in a high pitched squeal which caused her to grimace. She shook her arm to free it, but the Duke was unwilling to release her so easily.

"You must be aware," she said, "of my past association with him. It is no secret that he visited me nightly at Lambeth House and that he spoke of betrothal. I gave him my maidenhead."

Instantly his other hand sprang to her mouth and clasped over it. With a snake-like hiss he whispered in her ear, "It is the last time those words shall be spoken by you or any other person."

His fingers could not silence her and she bit and spit out between them, "Unhand me! What use do I have for a man who is thirty years my senior and of ill health? He is my King and I bow to his authority over England and the Church, but does that mean he has such power over me?"

Even Katheryn was startled at the strength of her outburst and had barely enough time to blink before the Duke's fist sent her to the floor sprawling at his feet. Before she had time to move, his foot came down hard upon her torso. Tears sprang to her eyes and she grabbed at her cheek already beginning to redden from the blow.

"Beware, dear niece, for I can squash you like a bug," the Duke said. He lifted his foot from her and straightened his sleeves and cap. I will inform the King of your great delight in offering yourself body and soul to the service of His Majesty." He punctuated with the delivery of a hard kick, and stormed from the room.

Four days after her encounter with the Duke, Katheryn was sent back to her grandmother's estate at Lambeth, and the Queen was sent away from Westminster. To give Anna an explanation for being exiled the King informed her, "The plague will kill you if you remain in London." Anna understood that the plague was not the real reason for her dismissal. She had been aware of the King's interest in Katheryn Howard.

The King journeyed across the Thames, sometimes as late as midnight, to visit his new love. The Duchess was beside herself with joy. She tottered back and forth in front of Katheryn and wagged her finger before her nose. "You speak quietly, with eyes cast downward at all times. Never speak unless asked to do so, and be brief with your answers."

Katheryn's face registered no emotion. "Do you hear me?" said the Duchess. "And not so much as a wrinkle in that pretty nose. He looks at you with loving eyes, and means to be rid of Queen Anna. He has taken a fancy to you, make no mistake about it. I shall tutor you in courtly manners and you will be Queen of England in no time." She placed her cold, leathery fingers underneath Katheryn's chin and squeezed. "If I had the opportunity to serve my King as his wife, I would not let it slip through my hands."

Katheryn stared at her in disbelief. "My cousin, Anne Boleyn, was given the opportunity to serve her King and she is dead now. What assurance is there that such a thing won't happen to me?"

"Anne was too headstrong, too smart. Although you are headstrong, nobody has ever accused you of having brains."

"I do not want to marry him."

"I have failed you," said the Duchess. "I have done you a grave disservice. Katheryn, we have no will of our own. Our duty is to fulfill the desires of the men who govern over us. That is as it should be. You are a willful child, but it's time you act as an adult."

Her failing eyesight gave her the impression that Katheryn's expression had softened and she lowered her voice to speak the next words. "Katheryn, it has always been that men rule the lives of women. The job of a woman is to obey the rule of men, and you will do as you are told. Tonight the King has requested you alone, to receive him in private chambers. His wish will be fulfilled." She motioned to the bed and nodded her head.

Katheryn shivered. She had been given a small room alone, a luxury compared to the usual Lambeth accommodations. Her uncle would visit her tonight after the Duchess had gone, to make certain the King would not be disappointed. It shamed Katheryn to be readied for him, like a mare awaiting the morning ride. The Duchess placed a long white gown on her body, and made certain her hair was loose and hung luxuriously down her back as the King had requested. He wanted to visit her here—hoping to keep the rendezvous as secret as possible.

Her mind settled briefly on Derehem. She wished it were he tonight. Almost immediately the image of Thomas Culpeper erased his memory, and although she had not tasted his flesh, she imagined it now and found it strangely soothing to her.

She lay in bed, still as death, when the Duke of Norfolk entered the room. Without a word between them, he brushed her hair behind her ear, and ran a finger beneath her chin. He stopped for a moment, as if to say something, but instead stared into her eyes with a look that served as warning. Then he was gone and the King entered without a knock. This surprised Katheryn and she sat up in bed and clutched the pillows to her chest. She expected an escort; yet again he was surprisingly vulnerable.

He knelt, supported by one hand on the edge of the bed, and bowed his head gallantly. She was overcome with wonder at this gesture and stared at his jewel-encrusted fingers that rested upon the covers. She remembered the last time that he touched her and the manner in which he squeezed her bosom and laid claim to her body.

"My Lord," she whispered, uncertain of what to say or do next. With difficulty Henry lifted himself from the floor and stood before her. He opened his robes to reveal his flesh—rotund and luminous in the moonlight. Horrified, Katheryn turned on her side away from him. Henry thought she was shy rather than repulsed by the aging mountain of manliness before her, and climbed into the bed. He cradled her from behind, and rocked ever so slightly, as he pressed his belly and hips into her tiny backside.

The body he presented to her was not the same one he saw in his own mind. The strong, manly chest of his twenties, thirties and even into his forties was no longer firm, but fleshy. The fingers had grown soft and thick, the legs swollen and unsure. But doubt did not enter Henry's mind, for he imagined himself a younger version come to court the fair maiden of his dreams. Katheryn's youthfulness awakened long forgotten instincts.

With his massive body pressed against her, never had she felt smaller and more fragile than now. His hot breath warmed her scalp. She waited for the feel of his erection against her buttock, but felt nothing but the repeated battering of his belly. He pulled on her arm and attempted to turn her body into his, but she resisted enough to make the action difficult.

"Do not be frightened, Katheryn. I shall not spoil your maidenhood. That must wait, for I plan to call you my wife. When you have taken your vows, then you shall know the full measure of my manliness."

Katheryn, turned now, her face pressed against his chest, felt him rub his lower body back and forth against her thighs. He searched for arousal and release without damaging her reputation. When her body could no longer stand the pressure of his continual grinding, she imagined she could feel Thomas Culpeper's muscular arms encircle her.

# CHAPTER 9

The sky was brilliant blue on June 10th, 1540. The sun annoyed the King during the May Day celebrations by disappearing frequently and giving way to showers, but now it shone without interruption.

Thomas Cromwell walked alone in the gardens, so concerned with personal difficulties that he made no note of the sun's return. Religious conservatives—the Duke of Norfolk, Bishop Gardiner, and The Earl of Southampton—had been plotting against him, and had called his Lutheran position on the reformation of the church 'sacramentarian heresy.'

This alone did not cause Thomas to pace the ground back and forth without pausing—it was the rumor that they had caught the King's ear. For ten years as Vicar General and Lord Privy Seal, Cromwell had been second only to King Henry, an intimate advisor to him on all matters, yet now he felt his previous influence dwindling.

"Damn." He spit through his teeth. "The King does not like the Queen Anna at all." He muttered and kicked the ground with the heel of his shoe. How could he know that Katheryn would catch the King's eye, while his choice for Henry, the Protestant Anna of Cleves, would cause such displeasure?

Norfolk and the entire Howard clan had opposed his Lutheran reformations. Now with Anna in disfavor and the King obsessed with the beautiful Katheryn, representative of the religious conservative faction, it seemed it was only a matter of time before both he and Anna found themselves in danger.

He wheeled about and began once again to pace back the way he had come. "Damn"—a blow to his back flung him forward, feet tripping, arms flailing. Before he had time to regain himself, Norfolk and the Earl of Southampton, surrounded by numerous of the King's guards, grabbed him one on each arm and locked on tightly.

"You are under arrest," said Norfolk.

Thomas Cromwell wrestled with his captors and freed his right arm. He snatched his hat from his head and threw it upon the ground in challenge. "I defy any man to name the traitor here among us."

"It is reported to the King that you mean, by arms if necessary, to enforce your Lutheran doctrines upon him," said the Earl.

"What man says this?" Cromwell shook his fist at Norfolk.

"What man does not say it?" Norfolk said. "Hold him," he shouted to the guards as Cromwell struggled.

Norfolk lifted the hanging figure of St. George from about Cromwell's neck. The Earl grabbed Cromwell's leg and pulled the garter from his knee. "You will no longer be requiring these. You have forsaken your right to wear these symbols of the highest order of knighthood. The Order of the Garter must be earned. Your deeds have proven you unworthy."

"It seems, my dear friend," said the Duke of Norfolk, "that your Lutheran Queen brought the King no pleasure, while our lovely Katheryn has been an endless source of enjoyment for His Majesty. You were a fool Cromwell, and the King's Court is no place for fools."

"I have done nothing," Cromwell said. "My advice was foolish, but not criminal. I will arrange for the King to be rid of Queen Anna. Tell him this and let him know my true intentions. I have never plotted against him, but have served him faithfully for many years. It is your evil words that have poisoned my position."

"Isn't it fitting, Cromwell, that your novel idea of death without a trial shall be used against you? The very Act of Attainder you drafted is now your downfall." The Earl of Southampton enjoyed the pained expression that flashed across Cromwell's face.

"Take him away," Norfolk said. "It won't be long before your 'Flanders Mare' will keep you company in the Tower."

No rain fell, and the morning of July 28th marked the sixtieth day the sun had shone without interruption. The fields were parched. Thomas Cromwell stepped from his cell. No trial, just as the Earl had predicted. He looked at his feet, but they seemed oddly detached from him now. They moved to a rhythm that matched his thoughts. "What did I do?" repeated over and over in time to the footfalls.

The brilliant sun shattered Katheryn's sleep. She awoke early on the morning of July 28th and blinked her eyes twice before remembering what day greeted her. She stretched both her arms and both her feet pointed gracefully. Her hips moved slightly side-to-side to loosen her stiff back. She recalled it was her wedding day only moments before she became aware of the warm blood that trickled down her thigh. She touched the place and lifted her finger to make certain she was not mistaken.

"A curse to be certain!" she muttered as she realized that the rumors of her being with child would soon be silenced. She remembered the night Henry penetrated her. Although in the beginning he had merely rubbed against her, or held her as a father might hold his child, there came a time when he rolled her over and put her on all fours like a dog. His enormous size became life threatening to her when placed above, and became a barrier to penetration when placed between them. Necessity had brought her backward, to her knees, and she trembled that first time, imagining the picture her rounded backside presented.

Then she wept. Tears fell upon the bedcovers, and his earlier tender mood turned lustful and his powerful arm held her down. He mistook her tears for those cried by a virgin, and when he had finished the task, he dried them with his rough fingertips.

"Do not cry, Katheryn, for in a week we shall be husband and wife. We have declared this to one another, so we are as wed in God's eyes. This is not sin." She did not answer him, but allowed herself to cry knowing that he would never guess her tears were those of hopelessness, and nothing more.

Pregnancy, she knew, would free her from this wifely duty and seal her position as Queen. A male heir would certainly keep her safe; it would have secured even Anna of Cleves. No male heir meant dishonor, even death. The blood now flowing from her womb would disappoint the court, and especially the King.

"Lady Rochford, bring me cloth pads. It seems God has not seen fit to bless me with child. I will be wed today, but the King shall have to be patient with his desire to fill my womb." Lady Rochford drew the curtains and helped her from her the bed. Immediately, as if called by silent messengers, Katheryn's room filled with servants, ready to assist and prepare the future Queen for marriage.

"A ship could sooner be rigged than Katheryn made ready," Lady Rochford said as she scanned the bodice, petticoat, farthingale hoop, gown, headpiece and jewels that stood ready to adorn the new Queen.

"Katheryn has no need of face powder," said her servant Katherine Tylney. "Her skin is of such purity."

"With her face painted and kohl about her eyes she will be exquisite," said Mary Norris.

Lady Rochford bent over until her face appeared in the mirror next to Katheryn's. Seeing herself in contrast to Katheryn's youthful beauty reminded her of how uncomfortable she was with her own looks. Her nose had always seemed to her the ultimate insult to her already plain features. Pinched and puckered it lengthened her face unattractively, finding relief only in the small bump that settled in the middle of it.

Katheryn's eyes moved from her face and traveled downward toward her bosom. Her nipples, barely uncovered by the dressing gown, were soft and smooth. Lady Rochford mentally compared them with her own wizened breasts and stared longingly at the lifted mounds of flesh.

"I know what is said behind my back: 'When too shall her head fall?'" Katheryn raised her eyes to meet Lady Rochford's. "Anna retains her head firmly upon her shoulders and I plan to accomplish the same. Today and tomorrow and ever more we shall dance and banquet and make merry. A youthful King is a happy and even-tempered one and I shall stroke his vanity so that he purrs as gently as a kitten."

"Not in time to save the life of Thomas Cromwell," said Mary. "Today he shall see the sharp end of the axe."

"God save his soul," whispered Katheryn. "God save my own."

Sweat poured down Cromwell's forehead onto his face. A drop landed at his feet and marked the ground a second before his footprint obscured it. It seemed impossible to him that his own feet were making this long walk to the block. Then it occurred to him—in a brief moment of enlightenment—that he now felt what countless others felt before him. Others he and the King had sent to their deaths. Did they too wonder what crime they had committed?

Beads of sweat continued to drop from his face in an endless stream.

He glanced up and saw the back of a guard leading him onward. Would the guard be happier when he was gone from this earth? Would he feel safer that this accused traitor had been removed? I am just another condemned body to him. Tonight he will eat and drink and feel a woman's flesh upon his own. Tonight my eyes will fill with worms, and maggots shall rest upon my tongue. Today the King weds his beloved 'rose without a thorn.' Today the religious conservatives have won the prize. Tomorrow perhaps fate shall swing in the opposite direction.

A shove interrupted his thoughts and he was thrust out into the brilliant sunshine, blinded and alone, he trembled as his eyes cleared and the executioner greeted him.

A trickle of sweat fell from behind Katheryn's right ear and began the journey down her neck. It was certain to be accompanied by many more before the day was through. July was hot, humid and the heavy garments left her weak and lightheaded.

Lady Rochford fanned her and lifted her skirt, allowing some air to rise up her legs. Katheryn felt the pinch of cramps in her abdomen, reminding her that her position—even on her wedding day as Queen Consort, was not secure.

The anger she felt toward her family for pushing her into this marriage with the King dissipated into resignation and detachment. Katheryn's mind floated freely from its encasement and began a rather pleasurable journey elsewhere.

As her feet moved toward the King, her thoughts recalled Lambeth and she fondly remembered her nights with Francis Derehem. A smile crossed her lips at the recollection and King Henry's heart gladdened at the sight.

Katheryn's eyes did not meet his. Instead she looked beyond him to a place in her memory—to the small bed where she and Francis first consummated their relationship. The remembrance sweetened with each step until, upon her arrival at the King's side, she realized that the simplicity of Francis' touch meant far more than all the diamonds and pearls that now surrounded her.

She felt suddenly that the King's pinched eyes had never seemed so cruel and lifeless nor the red jowls so weak and fattened. A rush of blood from her womb sickened her stomach. What if she should prove unable to bear him a son? Perhaps that was why the King had chosen a private ceremony to be performed at the Oatlands palace—quiet and obscure. It would then be easier to be rid of her should she prove barren.

Henry beamed with love and she managed a smile and lowered her eyes. How could she secure her position? Cromwell. He died today. A look of terror crossed her face, but her lips spoke the words, "…to be bonair and buxom in bed… 'til death us depart."

# CHAPTER 10

The barge moved slowly along the Thames toward Hampton Court, the King's country residence. August continued hot, and Katheryn was glad to be on her way to Hampton.

The afternoon sun illuminated the red palace in its warm glow and set off the beautiful brick façade, decorated with striking black crisscrosses. Elaborate chimneys, grouped four and five together, rose upward majestically toward the sky.

Although she could see only a small portion of the palace from the barge, she had heard much about its splendor: the kitchens that fed six hundred people two meals daily, and the courtyard clock with five dials, one of which predicted the tidal movement of the Thames so that all would know when to anticipate the arrival of the King's barge at high tide.

Katheryn spied thirty or forty servants standing at the dock, awaiting them. It was their duty to anticipate any and every need of their King and new Queen. It wasn't until she stepped out of the boat and looked toward her magnificent new home, that the importance of her position fully struck her. She was now the Queen of England, and all those who bowed, one after the other, were here to serve her.

She lifted her chin higher and opened her green eyes to the blue cloudless sky so that no one would be aware of the trembling in her chest, or notice the careful manner she placed her feet upon the earth. A misstep would diminish her position, and this first impression was an important one. She took a breath of the fresh country air, grateful for the breeze that cooled her moist cheek.

The Duke of Norfolk and Suffolk and the Earl of Southampton came forward to greet them and escort them to the palace. Katheryn relished the deep bow her uncle was forced to perform in her presence. "Your Majesty," sounded very good to her ears, especially when it came from his lips. She found she even had the strength to look him straight in the eye, and was surprised when his gaze was quickly averted from her. Perhaps being Queen had further advantages.

Over the moat and into the large center courtyard they moved—the swarm of groomsmen, ladies-in-waiting, and others of the royal household. Henry stopped and surveyed his surroundings. He loved Hampton Palace with its many towers and beautiful gardens and plentiful hunting grounds. Cardinal Wolsey had given it to him after the Cardinal had angered the King. An appeasement gift.

"Here take my home, it would make me very happy," said the Cardinal, and Henry took it gladly. (The Cardinal fell out of favor anyway and died on his way to trial for treason.) Upon acquisition Henry immediately made many improvements to the palace.

Perhaps his most cherished addition was the astronomical clock. It sat high above their heads on one of the inner towers of the courtyard. He stopped now to admire it.

Katheryn looked up and squinted against the bright August sun.

"It predicts the phases of the moon, as well as the tides and time of day. See the signs of the zodiac?" Henry pointed upward toward the bright blue and gold face.

"Your Majesty, it is in my sign is it not?" Katheryn asked.

"The lion indeed," laughed Henry.

"I shall be nineteen in one week," she added.

"It is said the lion is a fun-loving sign; eager for play and attention. Is that you, dear Katheryn?"

"When I am happy, yes. But when I am angered or sad," she hesitated and turned to face the King. "Beware!" She leaped at him playfully with her claws extended. "Grrr...!"

The courtiers gasped. Henry laughed. "Then it shall be the duty of all in attendance to make certain my Queen is happy and well cared for." He turned about slowly so that his eyes surveyed each and every person.

A murmur of "Yes, Your Majesty," filled the air.

"Good, now let us retire, dear Katheryn. We are hot and tired and in need of refreshment."

"Indeed," said Katheryn.

Henry declared the month of August be given over to banquets and hunting in honor of his new bride.

Two weeks after their marriage a celebration was being held in the Great Hall. Swan, goose, pheasant, quail, venison, mutton, tarts, custard, fritters, nuts, jellies, apples, and grapes were washed down with beer and ale.

The thick stone walls kept the room surprisingly cool, and the large pit in the center of the floor, which in winter housed the fire to warm the enormous hall, had been covered over to give more space for dining and dancing. After the feast the banquet tables were pushed aside at Katheryn's request, so that the dances might take place freely and without delay. The table where Henry, Katheryn and the highest-ranking courtiers sat was lifted above the others by a platform situated at one end of the room. The arrangement gave Henry a sweeping view of the festivities and most importantly of Katheryn as she danced.

Henry was proud of this room. The ceiling opened nearly sixty feet above his head. Cantilevered beams projected from the wall and supported elaborately braced trusses. The King's master carpenter designed the roof with pendants, arms and badges as well as a series of carved and painted heads that spied down upon the court. Bright tapestries adorned the walls, and picked up the blue, red and gold of the ceiling. With the help of seventy masons, forty-five carpenters, eighty-one bricklayers, twenty-one joiners and two hundred and eight laborers, Henry had managed to erase much of Cardinal Wolsey's influence and claim Hampton Palace as his own.

With buttocks firmly planted, legs spread wide, hands clasped over his enormous belly he watched his Katheryn caper through the dances. The fact that other men had to partner her—limited as he was by his girth and infirmities—did not concern him. She was by rights his, and even Henry was secure in the knowledge that no man would dare to steal his property right from under his nose.

Katheryn's gowns had doubled in weight with jewels and heavy fabrics since becoming Queen, and she found her endurance was taxed by the additional encumbrance.

"Katheryn, come here," said Henry as her dancing drew her near the table. His familiar address reminded the court of how different his relationship with this Queen was. "You would do well not to overtire yourself," he whispered in her ear as she leaned into him. "Your night's duties are just begun." He winked at her and she blushed. Henry's hands stayed on her body and he stroked her arm before moving them around her waist.

"Your Majesty, I see you are lighthearted this evening."

"It is enough to witness your happy face and the pleasure you take from dancing."

"Yes, My Lord."

"My heart shall be even lighter when I receive the news that you are with child," he continued.

Katheryn pressed her hands to her abdomen and released a nervous laugh. Her attendant, Katherine Tylney, fanned her furiously. "It is far too hot for dancing this evening." She glanced at Katheryn's stomach and raised her eyebrows. "An overtaxed womb is not a healthy one."

Katheryn stepped away from Henry's grasp and turned toward her lady-in-waiting. "Is my womb no longer my own?" She pushed the fan from her face. "When God sees fit to fill my womb with child it shall be done. Not one moment sooner. Until that time I wish to hear no further comments on the condition of my ability to bear a child..." she stopped and glanced in Henry's direction. A black look crossed his face and her servant moved away in horror.

"Your womb?" Henry rose up slowly. His swollen and tender leg gave him a sharp pain with the transfer of weight, and his eyes squinted momentarily in response. When they opened again Katheryn saw in them a look that caused her own knees to weaken. In his eyes now lived the man who destroyed wives, advisors, bishops and other "traitors" to the state. The man who stared at her now would have no trouble sending his new bride to the stake to burn. His eyes were hollow with rage.

Henry escorted Katheryn, like a naughty child, from the room. The courtiers watched. Even Katheryn was humbled—head hung low, dragged along by the mammoth and powerful hands. He spoke not a word until they arrived at his bedchamber. He shoved her inside.

"My Lord..." she began. "If I have offended you..." She went no further for Henry reached for her again and drew her into him easily manipulating her tiny body with one hand.

He placed his other hand about her throat. "Your body, your womb, is mine." He breathed into her face as spittle fell from his mouth and onto his chin. "And England's. Tonight you will remember who it is you serve."

His strong arms ripped at her headdress and stroked her long hair away from her face. "I want your hair loose, as a maid would have it." He pulled harder and harder and then leaned over to place his lips at her throat. Katheryn felt his bristly, wet chin against her tender skin.

"If I have offended..." she said.

"Were it any other," he said, "I would not be so understanding. You are young and foolish, but it is what caught my eye and continues to hold my heart. Make no mistake Katheryn, I love you or you would not be in my chambers right now."

"I meant no offense to My Lord or to England. I was merely angry at Lady Katherine."

"Kneel."

Katheryn obeyed.

"Look at me."

She raised her eyes to look at him.

"I offer myself in service to My Lord," Henry said and nodded his head to indicate that she should repeat after him.

"I offer myself in service." Her chin wobbled as she tried to hold back tears.

"It offends you to say such a simple phrase?"

"No, My Lord. Certainly not." Katheryn lowered her eyes.

Henry stormed to the door of his bedchamber and threw it open. Huddled on the other side were five women, and five men, all servants of the King and Queen. They had been waiting nervously, hoping for an indication of what was expected of them. They jumped backward, and to attention, as the door flew open.

"Lady Jane Rochford," the King said. Lady Jane stepped from the pack and curtsied, her head kept low. Without another word Henry stepped back into the room. Too frightened to move quickly, Lady Rochford hesitated, which caused the King to reach out and grab her roughly inside before he slammed the heavy door behind them.

Lady Rochford's eyes adjusted in the darkened room to the sight of Katheryn, kneeled, looking more a child of five than a Queen of nineteen; her slender shoulders drooped forward, her long thick hair fell about her.

"Rise Katheryn," the King said. Lady Rochford rushed to her side to lift her from the floor. She wondered what role she would be called to play.

"Remove her clothing."

Katheryn and Lady Rochford widened their eyes, genuinely stunned at his words.

"Your Majesty?" said Lady Rochford with a lift of her voice.

"Are you questioning my authority as well?" said the King so loudly that the servants huddled behind the door felt the vibration of his anger.

Lady Rochford raised her hands and began the arduous task of removing the Queen's attire. Henry stood back and stared at Katheryn as though she were a newly purchased work of art.

Katheryn, stunned at the request, steeled herself. The previously wobbly jaw clamped down hard and locked into place. She lifted her arms from her sides, and held them in the air, not only to assist Lady Rochford but also to show the King that no longer was she trembling at the sight of him. She fixed her eyes upon him and did not retreat when he stared back at her.

Henry, aware of the transformation of his bride, noticed a rumble of excitement deep within him. The only other woman who ever gave him this feeling was Anne Boleyn. He remembered Jane Seymour, the timid and gentle third wife whom he revered. He had felt more like a son to her than husband or lover.

Katheryn and Anne Boleyn thrilled him in the way he used to feel when he was a young man breaking in a wild horse. It was not compassion he felt as his anger melted away. It was lust, the lust of a primitive man. He circled Katheryn and noticed her muscles grow tighter and tighter. He felt the self-control that held her chin upright and her fingers steady. Lady Rochford was now merely an unseen force stripping away the layers of clothes upon the Queen's body.

The raised bumps of flesh upon Katheryn's skin thrilled the King. He leaned in and wrapped his large palm around Katheryn's waist. After the shoes were slipped from her feet and stockings were all that covered Katheryn, Henry pulled Lady Rochford away. "Have you ever seen such beauty?" he whispered in her ear.

"Never."

Henry waved his hand at Lady Rochford, indicating that her task was completed. With a bow she scurried from the room.

They stood now, one clothed in layers of brocade and velvet, jewels and cap—the other naked. Their wills met.

"I offer myself in service to the King," repeated Henry once more.

Katheryn hesitated, and Henry noticed a breath deep within her chest. Then her mouth opened and the words echoed back at him. "I offer myself in service to the King." She moved to the bed and lay down to await her master. Her open body was a defiant challenge.

Henry could no longer contain the urges rising up within him. He moved toward her, seated himself on the bed, and lowered his face to her soft, alabaster stomach. He waited for the feel of hardness against the weighty drape of his clothing.

He remained soft. When he looked into Katheryn's eyes they provoked him to mount her. He lowered his gaze away from her until they both stared at the soft place in his groin.

A silence descended until Henry could stand it no longer. "Do not forget whom you serve." He stood up quickly and exited the room with a bang of the door.

"The old bear looks tired." Francis Derehem turned to Edward Walgrave and rattled the coins in his palm. The sport of bear-baiting was one of Francis' favorites.

"Most likely he has no claws and his teeth have been pulled. I'm betting on the dogs," Edward replied.

The bear, tattered and toothless, was restrained by chains fastened around his neck. The chains were fastened to the ground by stakes. The three dogs, on the other hand, looked unruly and ready for a fight. They were large, two were brown and one was black and muscular. Francis counted the men who stood in a circle around the animals. "Thirty-nine. I'm betting on the bear."

Edward stared at him in disbelief. "The bear?"

Francis nodded and handed his coins to the bet collector.

"Makes no difference to me how a man wins or loses," said the bet collector and handed Francis three markers in exchange for the coins.

"I'm betting on the black dog. He'll be standing at the end. Look at him," said Edward.

"Not much to win on that bet," said Francis.

"Not so much to lose either," replied Edward.

At that moment the muzzles were removed from the dogs and the sound of barking silenced their conversation. The black dog pulled and writhed at the end of his tether and when the horn sounded he charged and seized the bear's throat before the other dogs were loose.

"Regret your decision?" asked Edward with a smug smile. He turned to his left and then to his right, but Francis had disappeared.

# CHAPTER 11

The yeasty smell of fresh baked rolls wafted through the air and into Katheryn's window. The autumn colors of the trees mixed in her imagination with the rich warmth of the bread and golden sunshine. She slept alone last night. The King was not well. It was the first time in two weeks that he had not come to her bed accompanied with great pomp by his men of the privy chamber. The great pomp, more often than not, led to little circumstance. She awoke with the smell, and a sense of freedom, happier than she had been in many days.

Although the King's mood had lightened, Katheryn now spent the majority of her time trying to appease him, fearful that his anger might, at any moment, be aroused once again. When he bed her, she disappeared inside herself. In fact, she had become quite expert at it, and he seemed unaware that she was repulsed by his physical body. He enjoyed cradling her as though she were a child; then speaking to her in mumbling tones about his trouble with this advisor or that ruler. He did not care about her reply—it was enough to voice his concerns freely to another.

It was during these late night sessions that Katheryn came to understand how uncertain and weak her husband really was. "They're all against me, Katheryn. They pretend to serve me. To obey me. To honor me. But in truth they wish me dead. I did not enjoy Cromwell's death. He was plotting against me." He would lay his head on her stomach—mumble and sigh.

He confused her. One moment he was angry and blustering, the next vulnerable and unsure—it was more than Katheryn could fathom. It was more than she ever wished to know.

The smell of the bread came stronger to her as Lady Rochford entered her room with a basket and a pint of ale for her breakfast. Lady Rochford knew how Katheryn enjoyed waking up slowly and lazily.

"He has asked to see you, Your Majesty. He feels poorly and requests that you attend to him. His doctors have failed him, he says. He asks that you come to his aid." She placed her breakfast upon the table and motioned for Katheryn to be seated. Katheryn wrinkled up her nose. Lady Rochford pretended not to notice.

"I shall go to him, but tell me, is his mood frightful or is he feeling rather benevolent today?"

"He is eager to see you. That is all I was told. After you eat I will make you ready."

Katheryn entered the King's Great Watching Chamber that preceded the entrance to his state apartments. She glanced up at the gold ceiling. It incorporated the arms and badges of the King with those of Jane Seymour. Jane died shortly after giving birth to the King's only son, Edward, and her reputation hung both literally and figuratively over Katheryn's head.

Accompanied by Lady Rochford, Katherine Tylney and Margaret Douglas, she nodded at the Yeoman of the Guard when he stepped aside to allow her passage. Huddled near the stained glass windows at the far end of the room were the members of the King's Privy Council. They had been banned from Henry's inner chambers, and they waited anxiously to hear on the King's condition both mental and physical. Katheryn glanced at the tapestries adorning the walls. Four of them represented the conflict between the Virtues and the Vices.

Her uncle was the first to notice Katheryn's entrance. The room was a large rectangle and the Duke was thirty feet from her, but Katheryn saw a slight smirk on his face before he lowered his body in a bow.

His action signaled the others to do the same and Katheryn paused to receive their greeting.

"I have been informed that the King wishes to see me," Katheryn said. She pushed her way past her uncle, and left her ladies behind. She opened the door to the King's bedchamber and Henry sat up in bed. His doctor was the only other person in the room.

The deep colors of the brocade bedcurtains—red, with blue and yellow accents—contrasted with his ashen white skin. This was the first time Katheryn had seen the King without a ruddy, pink complexion. He looked old and defeated. He had been complaining of sharp pain in his head and neck, and his ankles were swollen and tender to the touch—but he was alert, and brightened upon Katheryn's entrance.

"To look upon youth; I wish that I was young again." He reached out his hand to Katheryn and she drew near him and curtsied.

"Your Majesty."

"Leave us!" Henry said to the doctor. "You are useless. Katheryn's beauty is the medicine to make me well."

"Yes, Your Majesty." The doctor exited quickly, glad to be relieved, even if temporarily, of his responsibilities.

"How might I be of assistance?" Katheryn asked.

"Lay your hands upon my chest and place a kiss softly upon my aching head to draw out the pain."

Katheryn leaned forward and kissed him lightly. He smelled old to her—of vinegar and mustard.

"I must look an awful sight. I wanted to spare you a glimpse of me, but…" The King lowered his eyes.

"Your Majesty. You are my King. How may I best serve you?"

"Only your King? Not your husband?" Henry looked at her sadly. Katheryn was struck by how easily he crumbled when illness or doubt clouded his mind.

"Indeed my husband. I shall stroke your hands and feet if it will bring you relief from your pains."

Henry nodded. Katheryn sat beside him on the bed and held his right hand in both of hers.

"How delicate you are." Henry sighed. He laid his head back onto the large cushion and closed his eyes. His breathing was loud and raspy and a small bubble of spittle grew from the corner of his mouth. Katheryn looked away.

The doctor had drugged Henry with a powerful sleeping potion, and it took effect. Henry's breathing became more and more labored. She felt his grip loosen, and sensed him drift further and further away from her. Katheryn placed his hand gently upon the covers and rose up from the bed.

A portrait of Henry hung on the wall across from her. The picture showed him not corpulent, but handsome, young and eager, confident and proud. I understand why Catherine of Aragon fell so in love with him, thought Katheryn. She drew nearer to look at it more carefully. As a child she remembered hearing about the handsome prince who had grown to become the most powerful of English Kings.

A smell reached her nose and she turned back to Henry and made an ugly face in response to it. Sniffing the air a few more times, she moved toward the door, opened it, and signaled to the doctor.

"The Groom of the Stool will be needed," Katheryn said. "The King has soiled his bedclothes." She stepped aside to allow the doctor to enter.

Katheryn, dazed and distracted from her encounter with the King, detoured on her way back to her chambers. Her ladies kept their distance. Her walk took her outside, to the inner courtyard where she and Henry had, upon her arrival at Hampton Court, first paused to view the astronomical clock. A loud surge of voices broke into her consciousness. When she lifted her eyes she saw Sir Edmund Knyvet being dragged toward the kitchens.

"What is this here?" Katheryn asked. The guard paused at the sight of the Queen.

"He has been tried and sentenced, Your Majesty. He had a quarrel on the tennis court with your uncle, the Duke of Norfolk's, gentleman retainer—a Sir Thomas Clere. Punched him roundly in the nose he did. The King has decreed that such acts shall be punished. His hand is to be stricken from his body today." He bowed to excuse himself.

"Quarreled?" said Katheryn as she walked alongside them. "What prompted such a quarrel?"

"Tennis, Your Majesty," said the prisoner. "I requested that my left hand be taken so that my right might still do good service for the King. It seems my request fell upon deaf ears. I am to lose my right hand today."

"You say you punched Sir Thomas Clere? I suspect my uncle is behind this desire to see your hand taken. Your most useful hand at that," Katheryn said. She followed them indoors to the room beside the main kitchen where the punishment was to be performed.

Upon her entrance those gathered in the room stopped their conversations. They had never seen the Queen in this part of the palace before. "Your Majesty," said the startled group with a deep bow.

"It seems to me we have a great number of men for this simple task. The royal surgeon whose job it is to take the hand, I can understand. But the rest of you, what need is there of you?" She walked to the closest man and tapped his shoulder. Immediately he popped up into a vertical posture.

"The sergeant of the woodyard, Your Majesty. To supply the block upon which the hand will be placed."

On cue the next man lifted himself erect and declared his duty. "The master-cook, Your Majesty. To supply the execution knife."

"The sergeant farrier, Your Majesty. To supply the searing iron."

"The sergeant of the poultry, Your Majesty. To supply the cock whose head should also be struck upon the same block and with the same knife."

Katheryn nodded her head in amazement as one-by-one each recited the appropriate task. "And you?" she questioned the others.

"I am the yeoman of the scullery, with coal to heat the searing iron, Your Majesty. This here is the sergeant of the cellar. He is to supply the wine, beer and ale for the occasion."

Sir Edmund Knyvet paled at the recitation and Katheryn, seeing his ashen color, walked over to him. She paused a moment, placed a hand upon him and stroked his trembling shoulder.

"Be still. Do not fear. I have been with the King. I pleaded with him for your pardon and it is granted." She turned slowly about the room and eyed each man in turn. "Is there any here who is ready to argue with my statement?"

The guard's mouth opened but then shut quickly. Sir Edmund fell upon the ground and clutched Katheryn's hands.

"Your Majesty, if what you say is true, I am forever in your debt."

"It is true, now be gone, all of you. The King is ill and should any of you breathe a word of this to him I shall see to it that more than your hand will be taken." With that she turned her back on the scene.

# CHAPTER 12

As his illness subsided, Henry was reassured by the knowledge he had the full obedience of his Queen. Not long after the night he had stripped and tamed her, she had chosen the emblem of a rose with the words, "No Other Wish But His" and wore it on a scarf.

The New Year brought another round of banquets and parties. Anna of Cleves had managed to please everyone with the gracious manner she stepped down from the throne. For Christmas she presented Henry with an illuminated Book of Hours into which she inscribed the dedicatory words, 'I beseech Your Grace humbly when you look on this remember me. Your Grace's assured sister, Anne, the daughter of Cleves.' The gift eased his mind that he had done the correct thing in dealing generously with Anna. She seemed content with her new position, no longer as Queen, but as she had been titled, his 'Sister.'

Henry knew of Katheryn's feelings for Anna—the closeness that developed between them. What harm could there be in granting Katheryn's wish to have Anna join them for the banquet?

Katheryn rose from her seat and rushed suddenly to Anna's side. "I'm so happy to have you again next to me, dear sister," she said and placed a kiss upon her cheek. "I can say sister, can I not, now that my King has taken to calling you the same?'" She kissed her once more and returned to her chair, gleeful as a child.

"More wine, and more for Anna," she said and glanced at her husband to monitor his reaction. "My Lord, you look well this evening. You must take great delight in our company."

"Katheryn, come here." The King reached out his thick arm, and greasy fingers in her direction. "I am never so young as when you are near me." He grabbed her around her the waist, soiling her crimson velvet dress. "Stand back so that I may admire the gifts I gave you."

A necklace of diamonds, rubies and pearls graced her neck. Her head was adorned with rubies and diamonds. The candles reflected off her jewels and the King, overcome with her beauty, reached for her once again.

Katheryn moved closer to him. The court stared. They were entranced by the effect she had over him. He crushed her against the massive wooden chair, and she felt his foul breath and wet encrusted beard against her left cheek. "You have stirred the pot once again, and I shall be forgetting my dinner if this continues," Henry whispered in her ear.

Mary, Henry's daughter by his first wife, Catherine of Aragon, had joined them this evening for the celebration. It was Henry's desire to be rid of Mary's mother that led to England's break from the Catholic Church when the Pope would not grant him a divorce. Henry then declared himself head of both church and state and promptly granted himself the divorce.

Although Mary resented any woman who married the King after her poor beleaguered mother had been ousted, Katheryn presented an even greater problem—she was six years Mary's junior. And Mary, who had grown fond of Jane Seymour and Anna of Cleves despite herself, could not warm to Katheryn's extravagant nature. Mary rose from her chair, and scowled at the Queen. "With your permission, Your Majesty. I wish to retire." She managed a tight smile and a slight curtsey.

"Are you ill?" asked Henry.

"I am tired." She gave him a cold embrace before taking her leave.

Katheryn turned toward Anna to see her reaction to the King's attentions. She worried that perhaps Henry's disinterest in Anna, and his great interest in her, might hurt Anna's feelings.

Anna sank her teeth into a large piece of mutton and washed it down with her third glass of wine. She spilled a bit of it on her chin and wiped it away with the back of her hand. Her manners were also her own. Now that she wasn't Queen it didn't matter any longer.

For a moment Katheryn envied Anna's freedom. How wonderful it would be to move about without the watchful eyes of the court. A large fire warmed the room and the smoke made the air hazy. The wine flushed Katheryn's cheeks and she felt the heat rise in them. She drew a hand across her lips and brushed away the trace of Henry's kiss, making sure he did not notice. Anna did, and she smiled at Katheryn and winked at her. Katheryn's throat tightened and her head lightened. Was Anna trying to tell her something?

Katheryn walked over to Anna, drawn by the secretive way she looked at her.

"Dance with me, sister," Anna whispered as she approached. She reached out her hand, and Katheryn lifted her from her seat and they began a slow turn.

"Katheryn is the most graceful dancer in all of England," Henry said. "She will teach you a thing or two, Anna of Cleves. I am too old to keep up with her, but I have watched her many hours and I can tell you that there is no one to equal her." He leaned back in his chair and raised his goblet toward them before taking a large sip.

Anna circled round-and-round to follow Katheryn's path and soon they were both dizzy and giggling. Henry's head rolled backward and his eyes grew heavy. Then he roared with laughter at the two women.

"Stop!" Henry said. "You are making my head spin." But Katheryn did not. Instead she came toward him, turning and turning. He grabbed for her hand and missed. Anna of Cleves, drunk and giddy herself, attempted to copy Katheryn, but fell onto her bottom and shooed away the attendants when they tried to lift her.

"I dance like I play music," Anna said without a trace of vanity.

When he could stand Katheryn's teasing no longer, Henry rose with drunken difficulty from his seat and lunged toward her. His legs, weak from wine and illness, wobbled beneath him and three men rushed to his side to steady him.

"Get off of me," he said and shook his fists at them. They jumped back. Then they came close once again afraid he would fall and injure himself.

"My Lord, it is your safety that is our concern," Katheryn said and rolled her eyes and pursed her lips at him in the way she knew pleased him most. She laid her hands upon his massive chest and looked up into his eyes. "Perhaps you should rest now," she said softly.

Feeling rather foolish, but also rather ill, he agreed, and with a kiss on her forehead he allowed himself to be led away by the men of his privy chamber.

No sooner was he gone than Anna began to laugh. She grabbed her wine goblet and enjoyed yet another sip before putting the same goblet to Katheryn's lips. Their eyes met and Katheryn turned to the servants and other members of the court still in attendance and waved them away. "Leave us alone," she said harshly. "The Lady Anna and I wish to be alone. The Queens order you to be gone!"

When they hesitated, she rushed about the room and waved her hand at them. "The Queens wish to be alone. Go and leave us!" They exited, fearful of what she would say to the King lest they disobey her wishes.

"The Queens," Anna said. "That is rather wonderful."

"I suppose that has never been said before. Two Queens of England in the same room," Katheryn said when they were at last alone. "Anna, I've never seen you so relaxed. I think the wine releases the demon in you. The meek and quiet girl, who went away gracefully, has become something other tonight."

"I am learning about the pleasure of drink," Anna said. "I am learning even more about the pleasure of freedom. I am certain, dear Katheryn, there is no one else who would understand as well as you how good that freedom feels."

She reached out her hand and placed it gently around both of Katheryn's, so small were Katheryn's that both fit inside it. She drew her close and they danced back and forth across the room as though the music were still playing. The fire's light flashed across Katheryn's face and her full lips grew even more so in the excitement of such a strange moment.

"Tell me, Anna," she asked, "how did you do it? How did you free yourself from his grasp? Now you are a wealthy woman, you may do as you please. You remain in favor with the King and yet you are no longer his wife. Tell me your secret, sister dear." She whispered these treasonous words into her ear and felt her hot breath enter Anna and send a shiver through her body.

"Dear Katheryn, you care too much how men view you. It is your fatal flaw. Your desire to please them, and be pleased by them, is a trap. I do not have this desire and the King sensed this. He could not arouse himself to lust or love me, for indeed I care not that my charms are unseen by him or any other man. You are the only one who knows much about me, sister Queen. In this dangerous time it is not safe to let out all your secrets."

"Anna, I cannot make myself love him. I have tried for my own sake, but he has no attraction for me and I close my eyes and imagine another body against mine when I have to lie with him. It is torture and I only hope that soon I will be with child." Katheryn glanced around and lowered her voice even more. "I fear his fathering days are over."

Anna rubbed her hands on Katheryn's throat. Katheryn lifted her eyes to the ceiling. Forty feet above them she saw the carved and painted heads of the eavesdroppers peering down from the beams.

"Imagine it is my body that lies with you." Anna breathed into her neck. "We have no need of men to find pleasure."

Katheryn lifted her finger and pointed at the eavesdroppers. "The ceiling has ears," she warned.

Anna silenced her with a kiss.

Katheryn drew away from Anna. "All of us have secrets."

# CHAPTER 13

Henry's oozing leg and evil temper grew blacker each day. The veins throbbed, and a piece of bone, dead and chipped off years before in a riding accident, began its journey to the surface to erupt through his skin. Fever clouded his mind.

"Cromwell," he whispered. "The most faithful servant I ever had." His eyes scanned the nervous expressions and trembling bodies of those whose job it was to serve him. "The sinister faces surrounding me now," he said and waggled a broad finger about the room, "shall receive no mild treatment at my hands." No one dared to move, uncertain what erratic statement might next be uttered.

"I have an unhappy people to govern," continued the King, "I will shortly make them so poor that they will not have the boldness nor the power to oppose me."

"Yes, Your Majesty," the men of the privy chamber said simultaneously.

"Ahhh!" A wail arose from Henry and his face contorted as another jabbing pain gripped his leg. His hands seized a pillow next to him and he sank his fingers into it and twisted it round to release the agony.

His doctor cautiously neared the bed, unable to offer the King any real assistance, but afraid to appear uncaring. "Some sleeping powder might well soothe the King's pain," he whispered.

"Out of my sight!" said the King. "Out before I tear you limb from limb!" His arms flailed, his teeth clenched.

The doctor jumped backward and bowed before he raced from the room.

"Dark, dark it grows dark! Cromwell and my dear wife Jane are the only ones who truly care for me." Tears fell from the King's eyes and stained the pillow still clutched in his hands. No one drew breath or reminded him that the two people he just mentioned were both dead and one at his own hand.

Henry closed his eyes and his mind traveled to another time. He was young again, virile, and riding proudly atop his favorite horse. He imagined all eyes turned in his direction. His courtier's thoughts echoed his own—how magnificent the King is. Nothing could stop him in those days; he was as any King should be, truly invincible. A smile drew across his lips and the courtiers relaxed slightly, thinking him asleep.

His breath slowed and his chest rose and fell easily. He pictured his current wife, and remembered the day his eyes first set upon her. One glimpse and he felt the power of the earth draw up through his feet, giving his limbs strength and his heart warmth. She was truly his 'rose without a thorn.'

His mind wandered to dreams of her skin, and the picture of her rounded backside turned his direction. His leg was healthy then, and for a few brief moments he could be the young buck of his imagination. No one had been witness, but he knew that his skill as a lover had not totally left him. Of course Katheryn worshipped him. 'No other wish but His' was her favorite sentiment. Had she not had the statement embroidered upon her scarf?

The room stilled and the courtiers matched their own breathing to the King's, silently hoping to deepen this rare moment of serenity.

"The Queen is lovely," he murmured. "My lovely Katheryn, the rose." All heads nodded in agreement.

"Would the King like to receive the Queen?" said Thomas Paston.

Henry's eyes snapped open and looked in the direction of the voice. Everyone froze.

"What evil mind has suggested that the Queen see her husband in this ailing condition? I will not receive her until I have regained my strength." He put his head back down upon the pillow and closed his eyes. All the courtiers exhaled, thankful for such a short and mild outburst.

The only news of King Henry's condition to reach Katheryn was the daily report brought to her by her servants, or the ever-growing rumors of the court. "He is in ill-humor," whispered her lady, Katherine Tylney. Katheryn nodded and said a prayer, thanking God that the King had requested she stay away.

"I am bored," she said and stared from her window. It was a year earlier that her uncle brought news of her appointment to the court. "How much changes in a year. Spring will be upon us shortly. I wish to take a walk outside."

"Your Majesty," said Lady Rochford, "the weather is not so warm."

Katheryn glared at her. "I am bored and tired and if I stay one more moment inside I shall tear both of us to pieces!" Katheryn lifted her hands to the ceiling and screamed, unaware that the King's own screams were at the exact moment filling his room.

"It is your wish, Your Majesty," Lady Tylney said.

"It is my wish!" said the Queen, putting an end to any further discussion on the matter.

Once outside, everyone's spirits lightened. The sun's rays greeted the icy white faces of the ladies. Unconsciously, and simultaneously, they paused and raised their heads toward the warmth like a group of newly-hatched babies breathing in, for the first time, the Earth's fresh air.

More than the others, it freed Katheryn, striking a note deep within her soul, firing up the impish child that still resided in her. Her shoulders felt the weight of the heavy cloak and she pushed the hood from her head and stretched her arms high above her.

She screamed again, this time louder, longer and with deeper passion. The servants tittered, amused by their Queen's outburst. Katheryn spun around, arms outstretched, keeping the ladies at bay and uncertain of the proper response.

"Twirl with me! Dance with me!" She skipped lightly and brightly about and grabbed Lady Tylney's hands and pulled her along. Spying a tall, red-and-white striped pole with an elaborately carved dragon perched on top she grabbed hold and swung herself around it.

Suddenly, on the other side of the hedgerow, a flutter of wings, like a thousand doves rising together, filled the air with sound. Katheryn jumped and the ladies turned their heads to see what had made the noise.

"What fools have scared the birds?" a voice said from the bushes. Out from behind the shrubbery stepped Thomas Culpeper and two of the King's falconers. Upon seeing the Queen, the angry words froze in their throats and they bowed their heads quickly in apology. "Your Majesty, we had no idea!" said the frightened falconer.

Katheryn waved her hands at them and laughed. Her gaze landed upon Thomas, for although they had opportunities to glance at one another since her marriage, it was the first time they had been without the King's company.

Thomas boldly smiled at her and reached out his hand to offer her assistance. "Perhaps the Queen would enjoy an exhibition of the King's finest birds. Has Milady seen my hawk?"

"Your hawk, Master Culpeper? I haven't had the pleasure."

"It was given to me by the King himself, in appreciation of my service, shortly before your marriage," he replied. He led her along.

"I have no interest in cockfighting, Master Culpeper," she said.

"I have no intention of taking Your Majesty to the King's cockfighting pits. I would imagine it is grace and not muscle that you find of interest. The hawks and falcons are beautiful indeed." Thomas paused before the cages that housed the King's many birds.

Katherine Tylney came up behind and interjected herself between them. Thomas walked away, toward the birds. Katheryn could not keep her eyes from his body and her lips parted slightly as if wanting to speak.

"It is chilly," said Lady Tylney. "We should return." She glanced at the Queen hoping to interrupt what she feared was a reverie on the glory of Thomas' thighs. She could hardly blame her, and stole a peek at them herself. For a moment both women stared, and daydreamed about the specimen of manliness before them.

Lady Rochford, seeing what had befallen them, shook Katherine's arm. "It is chilly."

"I must be going," Katheryn said to Thomas. "My ladies worry over me so. They fear the cold presents a grave danger to my well-being. It seems one needs a more manly constitution to fend off the icy winds."

With no thought of the rumors that were certain to accompany the action, the Queen broke from her lady's arm and presented herself once again to Thomas. Thomas rushed to her side, took her hand, and bowed.

"Until we meet again," whispered Katheryn as he raised his eyes to her.

"Indeed, Your Majesty," he whispered in return.

The Duchess of Norfolk paused, squinted and looked down the garden path that led to the house. The sun was strong today, but she recognized the shadowy figure in the distance. "Is that Francis Derehem?" she asked her servant.

The servant girl snorted and shook her head. "Back from his piracy and smuggling," she whispered, hoping that she hadn't spoken too loudly and the old woman's deafness had spared her a scolding.

"Back from his journey to parts north," said the Duchess.

"Yes, Your Grace, I believe it is," said the servant.

Francis approached them and bowed.

"Francis Derehem, returned to Lambeth a wealthy man?" asked the Duchess.

"Robbed. Those scoundrels took everything. But, I was fortunate, they left me my horse."

"And your clothes. And your ring, I see," said the Duchess.

The servant looked at the ground and smiled. She knew of Francis' reputation for gambling.

Francis glanced down at his ring. "I had it hidden, Your Grace. You can't be too careful these days."

"No, I suppose not. But, I suspect you've heard the news, then."

"News?" asked Francis.

"Katheryn's marriage to the King."

"Katheryn who?"

"My granddaughter, of course."

"You mean my Katheryn? The King's decades older."

"All the better for him, I would say."

Francis looked at the servant. "It's true?"

She nodded.

The Duchess tugged on the girl's sleeve and turned from away from Francis. Francis stood motionless, his mouth slightly agape.

"Beg to her for money, not me," said the Duchess loudly.

"To Katheryn?" replied Francis.

"She is the Queen," said the old woman. She turned away from him and hesitated. She turned back toward Francis and said, "There was no precontract of marriage between the two of you. And no intimacy."

Francis furrowed his brow. "No intimacy?"

"Absolutely not. You have never known the Queen in such a manner."

# CHAPTER 14

"It seems like death around here since the King took ill. It shall do us all a world of good to attend the masque tonight," Katheryn said. "He refuses to grant me an audience, and he refuses to join us in the merry-making. So be it. The court shall make do without him then." She glanced over at her lady, Margaret Douglas. "And you shall make merry. It is too long since I have seen you smile."

"Yes, Your Majesty," Margaret said and forced a grin. She had just returned from the Abbey at Syon, where the King sent her for falling in love with Katheryn's brother Charles. "My heart is still heavy."

"That the King has pardoned you should be enough to lighten your load. My brother, Charles, loves you, but he was foolish to think that the King would allow you, his niece, to marry him. It was merely a few years ago that Lord Thomas Howard lost his life for marrying you without the King's consent. What was my brother thinking?"

"I took you for a woman in possession of a romantic heart," said Margaret. "I should have expected sympathy from you. Not condemnation."

"I have learned the hard way that no good shall ever come of a woman deciding her own fate where marriage is concerned. Certainly not a woman of your rank," Katheryn said gently. "My brother knows better than to put himself in jeopardy by falling in love with you without the King's blessing. It is over now and you must learn once again to be happy. Let me see your mask for tonight's ball."

Margaret placed a cat-like mask over her face and leaned in to the Queen. "It is the only way a man shall ever pay attention to me again. Should my identity be revealed, they all run quickly away. The King has seen to that. What fool would place himself in such a dangerous position as to find me, the King's niece, an attractive woman?"

Katheryn patted her hand. "Do not give up hope."

"No, dear Katheryn, I shall never smile again. Two lovers—two more than many women ever know—I have brought into my heart. And two lovers have been taken from me. I shan't try again." She lifted the mask from her face and a tear trickled down onto her cheek. "I am destined to be wed to an old, fat, bad-tempered man." A look of horror crossed her face when she realized what she had said to the Queen.

"Like me?" said Katheryn. "Is that what you mean?"

"Oh, no, Your Majesty," she said quickly.

"Never mind, Margaret. To be wed to such a man does not mean an end to the flirtation. You have much to learn."

Katheryn picked up her beautiful white-feathered mask and placed it over her face. Her gown was also white and feathered wings extended in beautiful drapes down her back and gave the illusion of a swan. Pearls had been sown into the bodice and along the neckline. "Now, let us go and enjoy the evening!"

The atmosphere was joyful, without the King presiding over the evening's festivities. Her uncle, the Duke of Norfolk, attempted to spread his dour righteousness over the event, but was largely ignored. Where all the others had costumed themselves for the occasion, the Duke remained in somber black robes, trimmed in ermine. When Katheryn and her ladies-in-waiting entered the room, a sweeping aside of bodies was the only indication that Her Majesty had arrived. Protocol was the King's domain, not Katheryn's.

She was radiant tonight. The King had been overly generous with her and diamonds adorned her neck. Immediately she was surrounded by a wave of adoring men; men who normally would dare only to admire her from a distance, now felt free to come closer, and breathe in her aroma. The attention puffed up Katheryn. This was what she dreamed of when the word Queen first passed her lips. This was what she had been denied since her marriage, what with attending to the King's aches and pains, or constantly being pawed over by him. At last she was free to shine. She flashed her most brilliant smile and reached her hand to Margaret to draw her into the circle.

"Gentlemen, this is a beautiful woman standing next to me. Her mask obscures only more beauty, not less." She lifted Margaret's hand and twirled her about to be admired. "I believe the young lady wishes to dance." She placed

Margaret's hand into that of a waiting courtier who led her to the dance floor. "Let your heart be young again," she whispered.

After Margaret departed, the circle of men closed in even tighter around Katheryn. Thomas Paston, who previously had been close to Katheryn only in his dreams, took her hand and boldly kissed the back of it. "Your Majesty, you look more beautiful tonight than ever. It is only a pity the King isn't here to witness the sight of you."

"How is the King? It has been a week since I have seen even a glimpse of him. I trust he feels much stronger with each passing day."

"Your Majesty, he calls out for you. First to see you, then to make certain you won't see him in his weakened state. His fever has abetted, but still he is wracked with pain," said Thomas Paston.

"Tell My Lord I send him my prayers for speedy recovery," Katheryn said.

Thomas Culpeper stepped in front of Paston. His mask obscured his eyes but the rest of him was fully recognizable to Katheryn. She pretended she did not know who he was and turned her back to him.

He spoke so that his breath warmed the nape of her neck. "Your Majesty, we meet sooner rather than later." She turned into him so that their bodies were dangerously close.

"Thomas Culpeper, I believe you dance, do you not?" She held out her hand and Thomas led her to the dance floor.

"It is shameful," Princess Mary whispered to Lady Rochford. "Just look at her. She behaves no better than a common harlot."

"You best quiet your tongue. The King will find no forgiveness in his heart should those words reach his ears," said Lady Rochford.

"I care not. She enrages me. I can no longer still my tongue. She is no better than her cousin Anne Boleyn and if she isn't careful the sword will find her neck as well. I say good riddance!"

"Princess Mary. You should not speak like this."

Mary's angry eyes reflected her words. Katheryn noticed. In response to Mary's black look, Katheryn giggled and reached out her hand to brush it coyly across Thomas' cheek. Mary's face burned and Katheryn smiled at her.

Suddenly, Mary pushed her way into the midst of the dancers and placed her hand firmly upon the Queen's wrist. Katheryn stopped dancing. Thomas stepped back. Slowly, the others followed suit. Katheryn, still breathing hard from the exertion of the dance, lifted the mask from her face and confronted

Mary. "Perhaps you mistook me for another," she said. "I hope, for your sake, this is so."

"This is what my father has come to. This is the filth he destroyed my mother for." Mary spat at her.

Katheryn was unmoved. "Perhaps, my poor deluded Mary, you have forgotten. I never knew your mother. But I assure you, I can make life very hard for you."

"How could I suffer any more indignity than I have already known? Anne, the whore-witch, destroyed my mother. My own father is determined to declare me a bastard. What could you possibly do to make my life any worse?"

"I will think of something," Katheryn said as she brushed past her and signaled the musicians to begin once again.

It was late. The dance was long over and Katheryn had retired to her chambers. She sat by candlelight and ran her fingers through her hair. She could not sleep, for the exhilaration of the night's events had not left her.

"I must see him," Katheryn said quietly to herself. She had dismissed everyone, but Lady Rochford, who sat in the corner, her hands folded at her waist, her eyes closed. Katheryn hopped from her bed and knelt down beside the dozing Lady. She hesitated, but a restlessness seized her and impulsively she shook Lady Rochford to waken her.

Startled, Lady Rochford flung her arms wide and in her panic knocked Katheryn to the ground. Opening her eyes to witness the Queen lying flat, she jumped to her feet and frantically pulled on Katheryn's arms to right her.

"Oh, Your Majesty! Are you hurt? Let me help you!" Still unsettled by her quick awakening she lowered herself closer to the stretched out body beneath her. Katheryn lay on the cold floor, a half smile upon her face. Suddenly, her lips mouthed the words, "I must see him."

Lady Rochford moved to the Queen's head and lifted her to a sitting position. "Your Majesty," she said once more. "Please forgive me, I had no notion what I was doing!"

This time, loud enough so that there would be no mistaking it, Katheryn said, "I must see him."

For perhaps half a minute neither one spoke. At last Lady Rochford whispered back to her, barely audible, "I understand."

# CHAPTER 15

The darkness suffocated Katheryn. Her bed curtains were fully drawn, and lying on her side, she curled her body into a ball and hugged her knees. Two days had passed since she whispered the treasonous words to Lady Rochford. Fear stuck like a fist in Katheryn's throat. She should have been quiet—there was no place for her to hide now. If Lady Rochford was not clever and made it known...Katheryn's mind did not wish to travel there.

Her ears detected a sound, and she lifted her head before she became aware that it was the pounding of her own heart. What if Lady Rochford was successful with Katheryn's mission? She imagined him alone, his warm fingers laying claim to her body. Rumors spread quickly. Her jaw tensed.

"I was a fool to trust her," she whispered aloud, "but it will be my word against hers. The King is still sickly and no one would dare to bother him with a silly rumor." The thought eased her tense muscles and allowed the memory of Thomas Culpeper to arise once more.

She squirmed deeper underneath the stiff covers. Her ears detected a sound. A drawn breath. So many enemies.

The Lutherans, and especially Archbishop Cranmer, would love to see her dead and buried. Hadn't they been plotting ever since her family's power had been restored? Anna of Cleves had seemed a ray of hope in their battle for power. Now that a Howard held the position of Queen they were angry once again. The noise stopped. Katheryn felt her fingernails dig grooves into her palms. "Where are my ladies?"

Slowly she wriggled her body to the far side of the bed, ready to flee if necessary. The heavy air, trapped inside the thick drapes seemed full of malice. The King always checked for knives stuck in his mattress. She had been careless, thinking herself too young and unimportant. Wasn't she now second in power? How stupid she had been. Never again would she be so naïve. Her left shoulder brushed the curtain. The tap, tap of footsteps circled the bed.

"Who's there?" She screamed as an arm thrust between the drapery and grabbed her roughly, shoving her to the mattress. Another hand clamped over her mouth and a face drew closer until she saw the eyes of Thomas Culpeper stare down at her. Her own eyes grew wider as he loosened his hand, and before she had time to draw a breath, he clamped his lips upon her mouth.

She felt his taut thighs—she so admired just days before—climb on top of her. His hard pelvis lowered down upon her own. Lifting away from her kiss he whispered, "I was informed of your needs, Your Majesty. I hope I do not disappoint you."

How they were removed, neither one remembered, but with the last article of clothing pulled away, Katheryn's naked body rolled about free and wild at last. A heaviness released from her chest and rose away from her. Her eyes blinked, as though clearing a fog that had for all this time clouded them, and a sigh escaped her lips.

Flesh and carnal desire lay beneath him now, and Thomas watched this with amazement. The action stirred something within him as well, but for him the sensation was housed in his lower body, an ache and a rumbling with the force of twenty steeds. He wanted not to capture the wild beauty beneath him, but to ride with her, sharing the sensations of skin and bone, sweat and saliva, smell and sweet salt.

This first night together there would be only an unleashing of their demons. Neither had ever found, before this moment, the perfect match to release the passionate core. Like lava spewing forth, Thomas felt the rush of his seed fill the womb of Henry VIII's beloved rose, and Katheryn's willing pelvis rose up to contain it.

When silence descended upon them, and they lay wrapped around one another, Katheryn prayed that a child would be planted inside her, and the King would no more need her at night.

In the morning Katheryn washed and scented her body to remove Thomas' smell, yet it remained housed in her hair. In private she drew a strand across her face and breathed in the aroma.

It was, she realized, a most dangerous time, yet instead of fear in her chest she felt only love and compassion. The King's recent absence from court due to illness and depression no longer had any hold over her—she was separate from him now, and more powerful, as though she too were in her rightful place. "Lady Rochford, bring my servant, Katherine Tylney, here."

Katherine came into her mistress' room with hesitation. Although close to the Queen, she was curious as to why she had been summoned when all others, save Lady Rochford, had been ordered away this morning. She sensed a strange charge in the air.

"Your Majesty?" she asked.

"Do you know Margaret Pole, the Countess of Salisbury? An elderly woman I believe."

"Of course, Your Majesty. She is in the Tower for treason, though it is said the King has nothing to fear from her. It is her relations that harbor treasonous thoughts."

"Queen Catherine of Aragon trusted her enough to forge a friendship with her, and at one time the King thought well enough of her to restore her title of Countess. It has come to my attention recently that she has languished in the Tower for two years with inadequate clothing and heating to protect her aged body," said the Queen.

"She is a Plantangenet," Katherine Tylney reminded her. "An enemy of the Tudor's."

"What real threat does Richard III's lineage pose to us now? She is old. I wish the tailor to make garments for her: a furred nightgown, a kirtle of worsted, a furred petticoat, a bonnet, hose, shoes and slippers. These shall be paid for from my own purse. You must see that they are sent to her."

"But, the King..." began Katherine Tylney.

"He will be informed of my decision, and he will give consent."

"Yes, Your Majesty." Lady Katherine was astonished by the Queen's order, and glanced toward Lady Rochford for an explanation. Lady Rochford merely smiled and shrugged her shoulders.

"Now go and inform the tailor of my wishes." Katheryn rose from her chair and walked to the bed. "I will also have Sir Thomas Wyatt set free. He has been placed in the Tower for ridiculous reasons. When the King is feeling stronger I will petition him."

Katheryn smoothed the covers on her bed and lay down. "Lady Rochford, am I not the Queen of England?"

"Of course, Your Majesty."

"I feel the Princess Mary has been insolent and a troublemaker. Arrange to have her favorite ladies sent from court. Leave her alone and surrounded only by strangers. Let her know I have arranged it. Perhaps then she will cease to meddle with me. Now leave me!" she said roughly. "Tell them I am tired today and need my rest. I wish to be alone."

His smell was still upon the covers and Katheryn needed it now. She closed her eyes to relive the previous night and draw strength from the memory of his body.

Her hands stroked her abdomen, and circled round and round, wishing for his child to be growing there.

"Please, dear God, give me a son," she whispered. "Give me a son so that I shall no longer be a weak consort upon the throne. Give me a son so that a part of Culpeper shall be with me always."

Katheryn stared at the letter she had just written. It took her the best part of the morning to pen it.

*"Master Culpeper, I heartily recommend me unto you, praying you send me word how that you do. It was showed me that you was sick, the which thing troubled me very much tell such time that I hear from you praying you to send me word how that you do, for I never longed so much for a thing as I do to see you and to speak with you, the which I trust shall be shortly now....when I think again that you shall depart from me again it makes my heart to die to think what fortune I have that I cannot be always in your company....praying you then that you will come when my Lady Rochford is here for then I shall be best at leisure to be at your commandment...I pray you to give me a horse for my man for I have much ado to get one and therefore I pray send me one by him and in so doing I am as I said afor, and thus I take my leave you trusting to see you shortly again and I would you was with me now that you might see what pain I take in writing to you.*

*Yours as long as life endures*

*Katheryn*

*One thing I had forgotten and that is to instruct my man to tarry here with me still for he says whatsomever you bid him he will do it."*

Finally satisfied that she had done her best, she sealed it and gave it to Lady Rochford for delivery. It was one week since Thomas came to her in the night. By now, the strength she drew initially from the encounter had dissipated into periods of fear and depression. There was only one cure for this torment, to see him again. The person to arrange it was Lady Rochford. Katheryn placed the sealed letter in her hands. "See it is delivered safely, and be careful, woman, with whom you speak."

Katheryn could not settle herself. She paced the room when word arrived that the King's health was improved and he had sent for her. Katheryn hardened her features to remove any traces of fear or guilt that might pass over them. She knelt at the King's bandaged feet and pretended to be unaware of the putrid stench emanating from the wound.

"My Lord. It pleases me greatly to see you much improved. It has been lonely without your presence to fill the halls and brighten my days."

Henry smiled at her, and placed his hand upon her shoulder. "The fever is abetted. I am strong now. It would do me well to see you smile and receive your kiss."

Katheryn stood and kissed him. "My Lord. We are all made glad by your recovery."

"I am well enough, in fact, that I am considering a northern tour. Never in my reign have I ventured further north than Boston. News of disloyalty in the northern counties has reached my ears. My advisors consider it expedient to venture outward to increase my popularity in those regions."

"Whatsoever My Lord desires, pleases me utmost," Katheryn said. She did not mention the fact that Henry's leg was still in need of constant attention, or that he could not put his full weight upon it. What entered her mind was how she would arrange her meetings with Culpeper while on tour, and a distant look came over her as she imagined how this might be accomplished. Henry, suddenly more concerned with politics than love, did not notice a change in his wife's demeanor.

"We will spare nothing. The people shall witness firsthand the splendor and might of their King and his new Queen."

The hour was well past midnight. Thomas Culpeper waited on the steps of the dark passageway and listened for the rustle of skirts. Not a sound greeted his ears and he took a few steps upward and listened once again. A door opened, and the scrape of feet against stone sounded below him. He pressed his back against the cold wall and held his breath.

"Master Culpeper," whispered Lady Rochford, "she is come."

He turned toward the voice and saw Katheryn, breathless, skirts clutched in her hands, race up the stairs. She threw her body at him and he opened his arms just in time to catch her and prevent the both of them from toppling.

"Oh, Thomas," she said. "I have almost died from longing." She grabbed on to bring flesh against flesh.

"Thoughts of your embrace have consumed me. I was lifted in spirits by your letter," he said.

The words weakened Katheryn, and she swooned. "When shall we lay together once more as man and wife?"

"Soon," he whispered in her ear.

"Thomas, the King speaks of a northern tour. What do you know of this?"

"It seems likely. Do not worry, your Lady shall be most helpful in arranging our meetings."

"I can't live without you."

"Your Majesty," whispered Lady Rochford. Katheryn turned to see her standing three steps below them. "I hear a noise."

"I cannot leave," whispered Katheryn.

"You must," Thomas said. "It won't be long. Look for me in your chambers."

Lady Rochford pulled on her skirts. "Hurry."

Thomas bounded up the stairs and disappeared down a long corridor.

# CHAPTER 16

On May 28, 1541, Katheryn awoke before dawn. The words of her favorite sonnet, by the poet Thomas Wyatt, turned over in her head.

> *Whoso list to hunt: I know where is a hind.*
> *But as for me, alas I may no more:*
> *The vain travail hath wearied me so sore,*
> *I am of them that farthest cometh behind.*
> *Yet may I by no means my wearied mind*
> *Draw from the deer, but as she fleeth afore*
> *Fainting I follow. I leave off therefore,*
> *Sithins in a net I seek to hold the wind.*
> *Who list to hunt, I put him out of doubt,*
> *As well as I may spend his time in vain,*
> *And graven in diamonds in letters plain*
> *There is written in her fair neck round*
> *About: 'Noli me tangere, for Caesar's I am,*
> *And wild for to hold, though I seem tame.*

Had he written it to Anne Boleyn, when both he and the King were expressing love, she wondered? Certainly to view Anne as a deer being hunted by the King, in love with Thomas Wyatt, but unable to refuse the amorous attentions of Henry VIII, was a theme Katheryn found familiar. Recently Katheryn's petition to the King had freed the poet from the Tower.

The Tower—that cold, damp depressing prison. Nausea turned her stomach and rose into her chest as she remembered Lady Salisbury. Today was the day she died. "I must attempt a final plea on behalf of the old woman. Her death is an injustice I can not tolerate."

Misty gray light filtered into the room and she realized that the Countess of Salisbury must be also awake counting the minutes, sickened by fear.

Henry was awake when Katheryn arrived at his bedchambers. He had not yet begun the arduous task of preparing for the day's activities. In two days they were to leave on the northern Tour. Today he would be busy with affairs of state. Katheryn threw such a fuss, that the men of his Privy Chamber feared keeping her out more than letting her in to see him. She rushed into the room.

"Your Majesty," she said, "you have shown yourself to be a generous ruler. When you agreed to pardon Thomas Wyatt at my request, the love and praise for us was boundless. Do the same for the elderly Countess and bear witness to the admiration that will flow, from your people, to you. I beg, as your most humble servant and loving wife, please pardon the old woman. She is no threat to you."

Katheryn, tears on her cheeks, hands clasped and wringing, turned her liquid eyes in his direction to strengthen the entreaty.

"No, I will not. The Plantangenets have taken hold in the north with recent uprisings. There are those who will not accept a Tudor upon the throne even to this day. To deal kindly with what is left of this ancient house will merely indicate that I have mercy and patience for such traitors. There is no hope for her, or anyone who associates with this rebellion. She must die." His jowls wobbled, and his eyes narrowed, but Katheryn pushed on.

"She is an elderly woman, frail and weakened by her time in the Tower. She has never associated herself with the rebellious ones in her lineage. She is indeed a relation to Richard III, and those who wrongly claim the throne, but she has never expressed a desire to occupy it herself, even though some case may be made for the validity of this. She is a loyal subject of the Crown, and praises you mightily. Please have mercy upon her soul and spare her." Katheryn was almost hysterical now, desperate to assist Lady Salisbury, even at risk to herself.

Henry rose, trembling with anger and grabbed her wrists. "Katheryn, I have been patient with your womanish causes. I have agreed with previous demands to pardon prisoners. But I warn you, once and only once—shut your mouth before you join her. I have spoken." He released her with a thrust that almost sent her to the floor. Terrified, Katheryn righted herself and ran from the room.

The baby's cries were sharp shrieks, interrupted periodically by coughs and gasps for air. Nobody, including the mother who cradled him in her arms, seemed to mind, much less notice. Perhaps it was the hot May sun in his eyes, or perhaps it was merely a bubble of gas working its way down a particularly curly tube of intestine; whatever the cause, the sound provided the perfect accompaniment for the day's events.

As promised, the Tower was cleared of all prisoners, and the townspeople were being treated to a fine display of Tudor justice. The one hundred and fifty people gathered were most interested in one death in particular—that of Margaret Pole, the elderly Countess of Salisbury. As she walked to her end, a low rumbling passed about the crowd. "How frail she is" and "Never mind the axe, one good shove should do the trick" could be heard among the voices.

Lady Salisbury was calm, but bewildered by all the commotion. She appeared to have no idea why she was here and what was in store for her. Her arm was so slender the guard's hand wrapped completely around it, even at its thickest point, and he loosened his grip, more afraid of breaking it in half, than supporting her should she faint. She managed a weak smile at the people who stood about with grimaced faces. The baby was silent now, as if sensing the need for all to register the horror of what they were about to witness.

The Countess looked at the young boy who was to be her executioner, a lad of no more than eighteen, almost as frail as herself. She smiled at him, a grandmotherly smile, and noticed his hands shook as they clutched the axe handle. No one had the heart to tell the elderly woman that this young boy had never before performed an execution of this type. The King's regular man was out today.

She brought her bony, brittle knees to the floor and fell forward onto the block. The axe was raised and began its descent as the baby let out a loud and painful wail. The audience and the executioner jumped in fright.

Bang! The axe missed the neck, and landed on her shoulders. The baby wailed louder—the old woman moaned and slumped. The executioner panicked. He raised the axe again, but too quickly this time and—bang—missed his mark. He brought it down three more times upon the old woman, hacking her to pieces as she died.

Hands shaking violently, he threw down the axe and moved away from the destroyed mass at his feet. The baby's cries had once again become quiet gasps for air, and for moments that seemed like hours, barely a sound was heard on the Tower Green. At last, Henry VIII was safe to begin the northern progress.

Five thousand horses carried an army of men and supplies. One thousand armed soldiers surrounded the King and Queen. The finest tapestries, attire, silver and jewels accompanied them. Little was left behind.

An endless supply of birds, fish, and doe were slaughtered along the way to feed the court. Two hundred tents were erected to house them, for no one, even the richest could provide accommodations for thousands of people.

Town-to-town and castle-to-castle the tour proceeded and all subjects under Tudor rule felt the presence of their Mighty Monarch and set their eyes, at last, upon their new Queen. Neither Katheryn, nor Henry, had ever seen the northern reaches of the English realm. The forests were thick and the people tall and fair. The further north they ventured, the more Katheryn felt they had entered another country entirely.

Eighty archers preceded Katheryn and Henry's entrance into the town of Lincoln, and behind them children, ladies and gentlemen, dressed in crimson and cloth of gold, followed. Church bells rang, and pennants decorated the town. Katheryn, stunning in her elaborate gown, was showered with praise and adoration. Rumors circulated that she might be with child. Many felt that it was this event that would at last earn her a coronation ceremony.

At Lincoln the bishop's palace adjacent to the cathedral served as the royal lodging. Upon Katheryn's orders, all ladies, save Lady Rochford, were barred from her chambers. This secretive behavior had become more and more commonplace, until Lady Rochford and occasionally Katheryn's maid-in-waiting, Katherine Tylney, were the only ones welcome at night. This behavior had begun a steady stream of hushed gossip among the court.

"Lady Rochford?" Katheryn whispered. She climbed the two flights of stairs that stood between her chambers and Lady Rochford's bedroom. The darkness heightened the uneasiness she felt. Her nose detected the smell of ale. A strong hand reached for her and a forceful voice whispered in her ear.

"Tell me you want me more than life itself. Better still, show me the same."

"Do with me what you will," she said. "I command myself unto you. You are my ruler, master of my body, heart and soul. Do with me what you will."

Katheryn's words inflamed Thomas. Together they pushed open Lady Rochford's door and tumbled into the room. Lady Rochford sat in the dark, waiting for them. She had expected their presence at any moment.

Katheryn and Thomas did not notice her. With a sweep of his hand he pushed the Queen upon the bed and lowered his body on top of her. "Do not move, Your Majesty. Prove your obedience to me."

Katheryn lay still, her eyes, accustomed now to the darkened room, watched as he lowered his face to her thigh and kissed it tenderly—stroking it with his lips, arousing her desire. She reached her hands to his head, but he ordered them still.

"Do not break your pledge to me, Katheryn. I alone command your movements." Thomas contained her body with his hands, relishing the ownership he now had over her. Power and lust combined to overwhelm him as he imagined filling her womb with an heir to the throne. He could be no more powerful than he was now, desired so fully by the Queen that her body rose almost unwillingly toward him.

Katheryn turned her face, opened her eyes and saw, inches from the bed, Lady Rochford. Thomas, sensing a change in Katheryn, turned his head as well and saw Lady Rochford. He reached his hand toward her.

"How long has it been since a man held onto those ancient breasts? Come here, woman, if you need a man's touch then ask, do not gawk like some stupid barnyard animal."

Lady Rochford leaned downward and presented her breast to Thomas' outstretched hand. He reached as though to fondle it and slowly opened his fingers around the sagging mound. Instead of a caress he gave it a hard squeeze and pushed her away.

"Be gone, foolish old lady. You think your dried up body holds interest when I have Katheryn beneath me?" He turned away from her and placed his lips upon Katheryn's full breast, as if to strengthen the point.

Startled, Lady Rochford retreated into a chair, and Thomas and Katheryn, once more covered by the darkness, ignored her. Alone she sat, and filled her senses with the vicarious pleasure of their moans.

# CHAPTER 17

❀

It felt as though red, hot coals had taken up residence in Katheryn's stomach. Her hands were cold with anticipation and her lips ached. She stood at the window—two days at Hatfield they had been—her gaze landed upon Thomas Culpeper. Her head tilted, her fingers lifted in greeting, she clutched her handkerchief tightly and waved it in his direction. Her eyes closed and a dreamy breath escaped her lips.

The courtiers noticed. All of them. Each lady-in-waiting noticed a change, but only Lady Rochford knew for certain the truth.

When did this insanity overwhelm the three of them?

Lady Rochford? Years before. She had been married to George Boleyn, Anne's brother. Had she really believed the lie of incest she threw at them? Or had her husband merely been an annoyance and his sister Anne an easy target? Either way, the accusation was taken seriously and they lost their heads together. Lady Rochford never shed a tear for her husband.

Thomas Culpeper's insanity was of a simpler kind. He was vain, privileged and beautiful. He lusted for power and women and was used to getting what he wanted. To make a cuckold of the King was dangerous. His hand raised in response to Katheryn's white handkerchief waving from the window.

Katheryn was a hungry adolescent, driven by a passionate need to create excitement, to feel fully alive, to stimulate her senses and free herself from bondage. A powerful force drove her, and Thomas fed it until it threatened to consume her.

A rhythm developed between the three of them. It began with longing, moved to whispered arrangements, ended in fulfillment and hasty good-byes which set up, once again, the longing. Each stage contained within it both unhappiness and satisfaction—the cycle repeated endlessly.

The northern progress had moved on and they were now in the town of Pontefract when Francis Derehem showed up unannounced. Katheryn had put Francis out of her mind long ago and was startled at the sight of him. This was the first time they had seen one another since her marriage.

He had come to Pontefract to petition the Queen for a position as her personal secretary, at the request of the Duchess of Norfolk.

Katheryn's worried brow relaxed with the memory of their love and brought back the carefree look of the girl so familiar to Francis.

Derehem smiled at the sight of her. He drew close. "How wonderful to see you," he said. The casual address caused the servant's eyebrows to raise and a glance to be exchanged among them.

"And you, Francis." She held out her hand to receive his kiss.

He lingered a bit too long then pulled away to study the jewels that decorated her hands and wrists. "You have done well for yourself, Your Majesty."

She detected cynicism in his tone. "Have you done as well?"

"I have neither the marriage, the title, nor the wealth and so I cannot purport to have accomplished much since last we met," he said.

"Leave us," Katheryn said suddenly. "All save Lady Rochford." Katheryn understood the necessity of at least one servant to be present should she need an alibi, but she was concerned to let others into the room, lest Francis speak a word of their past relationship.

When the courtiers had taken their leave, Katheryn pulled Francis further from Lady Rochford. "Take heed what words you speak," she whispered to him. "You may put us both in grave danger."

Francis freed himself from her and spoke loudly enough so that Lady Rochford might hear. "The Duchess of Norfolk has asked you to be good to me. I suspect you might feel that it is in your best interest to oblige the dear old lady. I welcome the opportunity to serve as personal secretary to the Queen."

Katheryn lay her hand upon his and dug her nails into it until a look of pain crossed his face. When he looked at her he saw an unfamiliar blackness in her eyes.

"I am happy to receive you into my personal service, Master Derehem. However," she leaned in closer to speak the next words in private, "should you be attempting to use your knowledge of our past relationship against me, I shall see to it that you are the one to suffer, not I." She pulled away and smiled falsely at him, then glanced toward Lady Rochford to show her that the expression she now flashed at Derehem was a peaceful one.

For a moment it occurred to Francis that perhaps this Katheryn was not the one he was so intimately familiar with. When she hissed, "I have the power to do it," he nodded his head and knelt before her.

"I humbly offer myself," he said.

"Rise," she said. "Leave now. Your appointment is assured."

The servants were too stiff and too quiet as Katheryn and Lady Rochford emerged from the room and swept past. They followed behind her, but she sensed the tension and judgment held in their bodies and minds. She lifted her chin higher in response, and stopped abruptly to turn and confront them. Katherine Tylney stumbled with surprise at the suddenness of the action, but Queen Katheryn said nothing.

She stood motionless for ten seconds and allowed her gaze to sweep over the group. She made it clear who held the power and whose job it was to serve. When she felt the shift in energy from being the judged to once again being the one who job it was to sit in judgment, she turned and raced down the hall toward her chambers. The servants hurried behind. Their footsteps created a sharp clattering at her back.

Lady Rochford brushed Katheryn's auburn hair with brisk, efficient strokes. She had never enjoyed the task of combing and plaiting the Queen's hair and there was no tenderness in her hands as she drew it tightly backwards from Katheryn's face. Katheryn was lost in her thoughts and spoke no words as the task was completed. Finally a last tug awakened her from her reverie and she remarked with little expression, "You are so talented with your fingers."

Lady Rochford bent over until her face appeared in the mirror alongside Katheryn's then brushed her fingers across Katheryn's cheek and slid her hand onto her throat before pausing just long enough to communicate something that resembled control.

"You know Master Derehem?" asked Lady Rochford.

"Yes," said Katheryn. She volunteered no further information.

"Well?" asked Lady Rochford.

"Yes," repeated the Queen. She rose from her chair and paced the room.

"You are concerned?"

Katheryn did not reply.

"We leave for York tomorrow," said Lady Rochford. "There have been rumors of your coronation in York."

"I am aware of these rumors. I am also aware that many people believe the coronation hinges on my belly housing an heir. Since my womb is barren I suspect the rumormongers will be silenced."

"Perhaps not barren for long," whispered Lady Rochford.

"Leave me! For God's sake, old woman, leave me to my peace!"

On their second day in the town of York, the King arranged to receive the traitors of the realm; men who had been accused of possibly harboring treasonous thoughts or participating in treasonous acts. Into the Great Hall a mass of the unwashed were paraded before the royal couple. Katheryn sat silently beside Henry, her face stern at the sight of these hundred or more men who had come to beg for the King's forgiveness.

"We wretches," she heard them say, "have heinously offended Your Majesty in the most detestable of offenses, disobedience and traitorous rebellion." Their pleas were greeted by the King's silence.

A monetary offering was laid at Henry's feet. One-by-one the men knelt. Then slowly they lowered themselves to the floor until all their bellies were upon it. Katheryn glanced at Henry, waiting for him to speak. Waiting for his pardon. Silence echoed about the large hall. Her heart pounded. Was it possible he would not forgive them? The room was still, except for the rasping breath and occasional coughs of the miserable subjects.

She too was uncomfortable. Her eyes moved slowly from body to body, until they became distinct and separate to her.

Henry did not move. He wished to inflict a period of uncertainty—to make the full impact of his ability to punish fall hard upon their backs. Katheryn squirmed. He was a cruel man. With one word he could have them put to death, or spare their lives.

The King moved and she breathed a sigh of relief. It was a sign they were forgiven.

A large feast had been planned for that evening. Katheryn entered the banquet hall and voices silenced as all eyes fixed upon her. Henry was so overwhelmed by the sight of his lovely Katheryn that he lifted his massive form from the large chair and extended his right hand in her direction.

Both Thomas Culpeper and Francis Derehem were in attendance tonight, and although Katheryn looked neither right nor left, she felt their presence. She sat beside the King. The table was laden with food.

Katheryn's nose detected a stench and she wondered if his leg was once again oozing pus, and whether his temper might soon follow suit. She raised a goblet to her lips and took a drink of the wine. Her appetite had left her.

Carefully, she lifted her gaze to scan the room. Francis Derehem sat, too comfortably she thought, as though he had been a part of the King's court since childhood. He flashed a smile at her, and quickly she diverted her gaze to Master John, her gentleman usher, to break the connection. He nodded politely in response. If he was aware of the signal sent to her by Francis, he did not show it. Instead he moved in closer, to anticipate her needs should the glance be a sign to him for assistance.

Katheryn continued her visual scan of the room. She saw Thomas Culpeper seated with the other members of the King's Privy Chamber. Her heart quickened and she felt flush with the knowledge that he was seated so close to her. Henry was in good spirits.

"I have done well today. The uprisings are being crushed and the traitors silenced. Although James of Scotland has not shown himself again this evening, it is the only dark spot on this successful mission. Tomorrow may explain his absence. Why should he be distrustful of me?" said the King to all those who were in earshot. "Am I not a peaceful man, an honest man, a man good to his word? It is true Scotland has been a difficult child to Father England, but I was hoping that James might change that with our meeting."

He glanced at Katheryn to catch her reaction. "But no politics tonight, for I am tired of James and his traitorous subjects. Tonight I share with my lovely Katheryn. Tonight we celebrate the beauty of my Queen."

Henry raised his goblet to signal a toast, and Katheryn saw that where Francis Derehem raised his too eagerly, Thomas Culpeper hesitated. This is where they differ, she thought. Thomas understood the danger and acted accordingly, but Francis saw only the glitter of the jewels and reacted as a child would, looking for admiration and attention from anyone who would take notice. Katheryn frowned and Henry turned to her.

"My compliment makes you unhappy?" he said.

"No, My Lord. Of course not. You always make me happy. It is merely a small pain in my stomach causing the look you take for unhappiness. It is gone now." Katheryn smiled and reassured him with a slight bow of her head.

Henry looked at her, and she knew the look. It was the one he gave her when he thought that perhaps she might be growing a child. When did they last have sexual relations? She could not recall. A week, a month? Her mind searched to bring up even the smallest detail of the encounter, but all she could remember was Thomas Culpeper breathing hot words into her ear. Oh Thomas, fill my womb. Tonight.

As though he had read her mind, Katheryn saw Thomas move closer and felt the blood rush from her face and head. She fell forward and hit her head on the table.

Henry gasped and the men and women of her chamber surrounded her instantly and frantically fanned her face. When she opened her eyes she saw in Henry's the hope that this was a sign of pregnancy.

"I am feeling poorly. Perhaps I should rest."

"Yes, rest, rest, dear Katheryn," the King said as she was lifted from her chair and escorted by her attendants from the room.

Francis Derehem remained seated, and Master John was not pleased. The Queen's Council had risen. He should do the same. He moved to Francis and grabbed him roughly by the arm to escort him from the room.

Outside the door, and earshot of the King, Master John derided Master Derehem. "It is disrespectful to remain seated when members of the Queen's Council have risen."

"I was one of the Queen's counsel before she knew you, and shall be there long after she has forgotten you!" Francis said and flashed him an insolent look.

Without hesitation Mr. John swung his fist at Derehem's face and smashed him roundly on the chin.

Derehem returned the blow, and being the younger man, sent Master John onto his back before he could defend himself.

"The King shall hear of this!" The elder man cursed him loudly. Francis walked away.

# CHAPTER 18

Katheryn heard the Duke of Norfolk's voice all the way down the hall. "One hundred lovers," he said as she approached the open door to the King's outer chamber. "One hundred lovers could not satisfy the evil witch."

He was talking about her cousin, Anne Boleyn. "Her maidenhead had been sold to the Devil long before she at last offered herself to Your Majesty. Anna of Cleves..." the Duke paused, suddenly uncertain which point of view was the politically correct one to take about Anna at the moment. Was Anna supposed to be a virgin as the annulment claimed, allowing the King to divorce her? Or was she used property, made clear to the King that first night by the state of her saggy breasts and so providing a perfect excuse for him to dismiss his wife?

Katheryn listened to her uncle in disbelief. Although she hated him personally she had always admired the slick way he manipulated Henry's enormous vanity—kissing and bowing just enough to appear unwavering in his loyalty but never so much to play the bumbling, groveling fool.

Norfolk's delicate dance of destroying his enemies and winning the favor of the fickle King was well known. He was hated, but admired for his iron smoothness. Yet here he was, beads of sweat erupting on his face, a shiver in his spine and foolishly entering into the only subject more dangerous than religion, Henry's marriages.

The Duke swallowed and pulled on his collar. "Her virtue...,"

"Silence," interrupted the King. "I have titled her Sister." He turned his attention to Katheryn as she appeared in the doorway. "Of Katheryn there is no doubt."

At the same moment Norfolk was rescued by this one statement, Katheryn realized fully, for the first time, she was as good as dead. Not even the King truly believed that Anne Boleyn had been unfaithful. Yet many people had been willing to persecute her, and call her a witch to remain in favor with Henry when he wanted to be rid of her.

Katheryn was far less virtuous, and many knew it. Even Norfolk, as he agreed now with the King's assessment of her virtue, knew he was lying. How quickly would he change his mind should it serve him to do so?

No coronation had been scheduled for York. Her belly remained empty. It was inevitable that she too would die, save for one thing. A son. Only a male child could save her life.

The court had tarried in York for a few weeks. As time went by and talk of her coronation faded, Katheryn grew more and more obsessed with thoughts of pregnancy. Tonight she awaited the King. As always her hair was long and hung about her shoulders and her gown draped the way the King liked it. Tonight the coupling must be successful. How she would accomplish this?

She remembered the last time he laid with her he was flaccid and feeling unwell. Should she become pregnant with Thomas Culpeper's child now, there would be grave doubt in the King's mind about the father of the child. She could not let that happen. She knew what she must do.

Henry arrived on his own two legs, but with difficulty. He had taken to being carried at times, especially up and down stairs, but in order to retain the image of himself as virile prince he had come to court Katheryn under his own power. He studied her, hands on hips, legs astride—a pose Katheryn had become familiar with. A pose he favored for the strength it gave him. Tonight she matched his gaze and stared deeply into the dark gray eyes, narrowed by surrounding fat. She saw fully the thin lips, and the lightly whiskered chin that hid, only slightly, the other two beneath it.

"My Lord," she whispered. She rose from her chair and reached her hands to him, allowing the dressing gown to fall from her shoulder and reveal her flesh beneath it. She drew it together with her fingers to hide her nakedness. This must not happen too fast or I will be disappointed.

"My Lord, sit down and be comfortable." She moved aside and he lowered his large body into the wooden chair, which fortunately had been carved with arms that curved around his bulk. Katheryn knelt at his feet and removed his slippers. The skin was stretched and pulled about the swollen, purple ankles, and she noticed that sores had once again erupted on his calf. With gentle fingers she stroked upward from the swollen toes to relieve the pressure and pain of which he constantly complained. She made certain that in her kneeling and bending her dressing gown opened just enough to reveal the flesh which lay beneath it, but closed enough to pretend at innocence.

Henry shut his eyes. Slowly Katheryn allowed her fingers to rise higher on his leg, and bit her lip to obscure any distaste that might appear on her face. Her hands traveled to his crotch, but stopped before reaching their mark. Henry allowed a small sound to pass his lips.

She decided that tonight she would be on top of him. A position she had never before dared to assume with the King—but one that put her in control. She realized the possibility of offending him with this aggressiveness—but felt certain it was the only way to guarantee a successful coupling. If the act was fulfilled satisfactorily, all other thoughts would be erased from the King's mind—even those that might lead him to question where a virgin, prior to bedding him, had learned so bold a move.

Henry's eyes opened and without moving his head, now thrown backward, he looked downward toward her. He was still now, and Katheryn's heart raced with fear. She felt suddenly that she was putting her hand in a lion's cage, hoping that her soothing words and soft strokes would render it as peaceful as a kitty.

Henry did not move. His breath was strained and his mouth opened to receive enough oxygen to fill his massive chest. The sound filled Katheryn's head—in and out the rasping breaths drew her closer and closer. She lifted her tiny body up and straddled him, placing one leg on either side, slipping it through the rungs of the large chair. She felt Henry's pelvis move slightly, and she relaxed, daring to match her own with its rhythm. She wondered if any other Queen dared such a move. Certainly not the prudish Jane Seymour, nor the pious Catherine of Aragon. Perhaps Anne Boleyn, one day as she sat on his lap, had moved her body to his.

She looked into his face and saw a sharp stab of pain register across it. Her plan was failing. She lifted her body from the chair, swung her feet onto the floor, and laughed as she drew her hands across his cheek to take his mind from his wounds.

He grabbed her wrist with a power that, should she resist, would break it. Still he was silent, and his silence threatened her more than any words he might speak. There was no tenderness in him now; she had unleashed the same animal she witnessed that day she stood stripped, naked and vulnerable before him. He tore the robe from her body. "You have climbed upon the King," he said suddenly. She shivered. "And the King has liked it." He laughed.

Feeling his power once again restored, he rose and led Katheryn to the bed. Lying down upon his back he said "Is this what my Katheryn suggests? That she mount her King like a rider mounts his horse?" The King laughed again.

Katheryn was afraid to relax, afraid that his humor might change at any moment. Cautiously she got into bed, thinking how appalled the court would be by her strange behavior.

"I think I should enjoy a new ride," said Henry. Dutifully, Katheryn mounted him and moved up and down. Henry giggled like a young boy playing a new game.

Katheryn's hands found his penis and feeling it becoming a consistency she could use, slipped it inside of her and prayed that it would release a rush of royal fluid.

In a few minutes a shudder and moan indicated success, and Katheryn dismounted. Soon the King's moan became a raspy breath, and the raspy breath soon turned louder into a snore and Katheryn lay quietly beside the King, once again praying for her life.

# CHAPTER 19

Mary Lascelles Hall sniffed and pressed a handkerchief to her nose. Always red, and usually runny, it contributed to the opinion others held of her as dour, upright and without joy. She liked this facade she broadcast, and nursed it continually by passing judgment on those around her. Others never met her high standards. She had not seen Katheryn since Lambeth, and she didn't like her then and she certainly had no love for her now that she was Queen of England. She put down her needlepoint, and stared at her brother John in disbelief.

"What use do I have of Katheryn Howard?" She snorted. "She was loose and sinful since the day she was born. I should no sooner serve in her court than pay homage to the Devil himself. The way she carried on at Lambeth—and her, an unmarried woman! Nightly Francis Derehem would visit and they would huff and blow behind the bed curtains, that only a fool would wonder what was going on behind there. She lost her maidenhead long before she sold herself to the King. Evil she is and evil she will die."

John wheeled about and placed his hand upon his sister Mary's shoulder. "My God, Mary, is what you tell me truth? Why have you not spoken of it before?"

"You had not suggested I grovel to her for employment before this. I have my pride, dear brother."

"Then the King is being taken for a fool. I'd bet my life that the Duke of Norfolk is behind this charade and his conservative cronies with him. Since Cromwell died they've done nothing but gloat about their restored power. Now I will bring them to their knees with this information."

"Beware, the King will have your head upon the block should he suspect lies and treason. He loves her they say. He loves her more than the others. Perhaps you should abandon this idea and let another man take her down," said Mary.

"Perhaps," he said. "Perhaps not. It seems to me that you could pass this information along, with no danger to yourself. It is the truth after all."

"Of course, it is the truth. I have no reason to lie about such things."

"Then I believe it is your duty to inform the Archbishop. He will know what to do with the information." John studied his sister's face to see what her reaction would be to this idea.

"I could do that, if you believe it is my duty."

Archbishop Cranmer sat before Mary Lascelles Hall and nodded politely. The moment he first met her he did not like her. Her righteousness irritated him. When he realized that he too had probably been accused of possessing the same trait, his repulsion for her grew so enormous that he thought for a brief moment of dismissing her.

Instead he sat quietly and nodded, thinking of the sharp contrast she provided to Katheryn Howard, the woman she now accused of heinous crimes.

"Mr. Henry Mannox had no right to be affiancing himself to a daughter of the Howards," Mary said, "and I told him just that. Why, I said, do you not know that if the Duchess knew of the love between you she would undo you? Katheryn is of a noble house, and if you marry her, some of her blood will kill thee! That is what I told Mr. Mannox."

Archbishop Cranmer nodded politely.

"And do you know what he said to me? Why he told me that his designs were of a dishonest kind. Right those words he used. He said that Katheryn told him he should have her maidenhead, though it be painful to her. I told him to be gone with his empty promises of marriage. But I doubt not that Mr. Mannox has known her intimately."

With the mention of Katheryn's virginity, Archbishop Cranmer smiled. He had always admired Katheryn's beauty and fire. He looked at Mary and thought of her maidenhead being given up. It put a scowl on his face as he shook his head to clear the image.

"Terrible, isn't it?" Mary agreed, thinking the gesture directed in shame toward Katheryn.

"Yes," said Cranmer. "Terrible."

"And that is only the beginning. Hear what I say about Master Francis Dereham. For a hundred nights or more he crept into the ladies dormitory. If Master Mannox had not taken her maidenhead, then Master Derehem most certainly did, for the noises that were made behind the curtains even a child would understand the meaning of. As I have said from the first moment the news reached my ears, I am sorry the King ever married the Queen." Mary folded her hands in her lap and exhaled to indicate that she had said enough.

"You understand the seriousness of your accusation? If the Queen was pre-contracted to either of these men then her marriage to the King is automatically invalid. If she was loose before she married the King…He drifted off.

Mary finished the sentence for him. "Then she has been loose after."

"You are a Protestant?" Cranmer asked.

"Why do you ask?" She looked at him with suspicion. "I am no heretic. It is well known I have no love for the Howards, especially the Duke of Norfolk. But I am a loyal woman to the King, and not a heretic!"

Archbishop Cranmer nodded his head and rose to signal the discussion had reached an end. He knew what he must do.

Katheryn had been summoned to the King's chambers and then left alone. She felt uneasy, but brushed it off with a wave of her hand and moved across the room to the King's writing table. Upon it sat his seal, and a book. Her fingers ran over the book, and she turned it around to see the title. "The Protestant—" she said as she lifted the cover, but a hand crashed down and slammed it shut, before her finger had time to escape. Frightened, she jumped backward directly onto the King's aching foot.

Simultaneously they let out a scream. The beautiful brooch the King had been carrying in his hands landed with a thud upon the floor.

"My Lord!" Katheryn said.

"AHHH!" the King said. He hobbled to the chair and plopped down, raising his leg in an attempt to ease the pain.

"Oh, My Lord. I had no idea."

"You are careless, Katheryn."

She backed away, uncertain about what action would appease him the most—caring for the injured leg, or keeping her distance. Henry scowled and looked at the brooch now lying face down on the floor between them.

"Pick it up!" Katheryn followed his gaze until it landed upon the brooch. With trembling hands she reached for it. It was stunning. Set with thirty-five diamonds and eighteen rubies it depicted the story of Noah. Her bottom lip also trembled, and she let a tear slide from the corner of her eye. Like a child she handed it to him, while casting her eyes downward.

"Come here, Katheryn. It is for you. Let me dry your tears." He touched the drop and wiped it gently away. Katheryn smiled and with her eyes still averted, rubbed her shoulder into his arm, like a cat around the legs of its owner.

"It is for me? It is beautiful."

"Indeed. You do have the power to soften my heart, and my will. Let me put it on you." Henry fastened the jewels to her bodice and pushed her away so that he might get a better look. "Move, Katheryn, that I might see it shine in the light."

Katheryn swayed back-and-forth and circled slowly about the room, moving her hands and arms and torso gracefully for the King to admire.

"It pleases you, My Lord?" She watched Henry's head sway side-to-side. Her body charmed him as though he were a snake and she the flute. Henry did not answer, but reached out toward her and moved his index finger to reel her in closer.

"Do not be angry with me, My Lord. It frightens me." Katheryn was near enough now that his finger just barely brushed the fabric of her skirt.

Henry smiled and grabbed the cloth between two fingers to hold her still. "If you knew the spell you cast upon me, Katheryn, you would never fear me again. It is me that is a child in your presence. You frighten me, for I am weak, and only you can make me strong again."

"And how might I accomplish this?" The sassiness returned to her voice now that she knew the King had succumbed.

"Tonight I will be the horse and you the rider." He grinned.

"The King enjoyed my little game?"

"The King wishes to be saddled."

Archbishop Cranmer was tired. His long, pinched nose accentuated his sad, downcast eyes. The black hat upon his head covered his ears and made his long face seem even longer. His cloak appeared weighty upon his thin back. It was said he had a wife, married during the brief period when Henry VIII looked favorably upon marriage in the clergy and abandoned when the King changed his mind. His heavy heart stared at the letter before him. It was cold today, his fingers were stiff and his knees ached.

He turned his gaze from the letter and stared out the window. How long before the King returned from his northern tour? Weeks perhaps? John Lascelles had sworn to him that his sister would not lie about such matters. Still, whosoever passed this news to the King risked his own neck. Cranmer, not yet recovered from the death of his Protestant friend Cromwell, rubbed his hand back and forth across his throat.

"I should feel nothing but joy at this task. My opportunity to bring down the Duke and his conservative friends. Yet my heart feels only sadness. How many Queens must the King have before we all tire of this endless struggle for power? She will die, or I will die. Which shall it be this time?"

Although unfinished with writing the terrible truth about Queen Katheryn, Cranmer rose and walked about the room circling the desk like a hawk. Three, four, five times he circled, pen in hand. "It is a loathsome duty. One that must be done."

He walked to the fire and reached his fingers in above the flames. An ember fell, snapped and sizzled. He watched it until it was nothing but gray ash. When the ash was swept upward in the draft he turned away and shuffled back to his desk.

"Sometimes men burn," he said. "Sometimes men burn. Their souls rise to God, their bodies return to the Earth. While on the Earth, they serve—God, country, King—it matters not. In the end..." he looked back at the fire and then to the incomplete letter. He wrote the words: *Laid nightly with a Francis Derehem.*

Katheryn, asleep upon the King's bed, rolled over and mumbled. Her hand reached out and landed upon an empty space beside her. Slowly she opened her eyes and scanned the room, trying to remember where she was, and how she arrived there. Her ears detected a whisper in the failing light and she lifted her head to locate the owner of the voice.

The King knelt beside the bed with his head bowed in prayer. "I render thanks to Thee, O Lord, that after so many strange accidents that have befallen my marriages thou hast been pleased to give me a wife so entirely conformed to my inclinations as her I now have." Katheryn held her breath and lowered herself slowly back onto the bed, hoping to go unnoticed.

She heard a moan as the King stood up, and then the shuffling of feet as he moved slowly around the bed and stopped beside her. She did not move and barely breathed.

"I will make a public announcement," she heard him say. "On November 1st in the Chapel Royal I will bless my rose without a thorn," my lovely Katheryn, and declare that in all churches throughout the land, all my subjects must pay similar honor to my Queen and her virtues."

Katheryn's heart raced. "All shall know the purity that is Katheryn. All shall know that when you give me a male heir, the boy's mother, is an angel." Henry stood beside the bed, and watched her sleep, tracing her lips, cheek and chin with his eyes. "You are beautiful," he whispered, as a rebel tear formed in the corner of his eye and fell down his face.

Culpeper paused in the courtyard and glanced up at the Queen's dark window. Was she with the King tonight? It had been over a week since they had been alone together. Only yesterday while assisting the King's dresser he found himself thinking about Katheryn—he had pressed his lips together tightly to be certain her name would not pass them. It was foolish, but lately he found himself quite frightened of such a slip.

Footsteps, with an urgency that signaled danger, sounded at his back, and he grabbed the hilt of his sword. A hand clasped his shoulder. "Who are you? I have no business with you."

"But, I have business with you, Culpeper," replied Francis. "I demand to know your intentions with Katheryn."

"Katheryn?" asked Culpeper and stepped back to shake himself loose from Francis.

"I have seen the glances between you."

"Are you mad?"

"I am familiar with Katheryn's looks of affection. It was not so long ago that I was the recipient."

"Lower your voice."

"It is a dangerous game you play," said Francis.

"Dangerous? The King has put his trust in me."

"It is not the King who threatens you," said Francis and moved in closer to Culpeper. They were chest-to-chest, now. Francis was the taller and Culpeper drew himself up to full height.

"You are threatening me to stop looking at the Queen because you think she belongs to you?" asked Culpeper incredulously.

"Katheryn's heart belongs to me," said Francis.

"I think the King would disagree with you."

"This is my warning, Culpeper. I give only one." Francis turned his back on him.

Culpeper, amazed by the encounter, watched Francis walk away into the darkness.

# CHAPTER 20

Back in Hampton Court, five months after the northern progress first began; Katheryn was again in familiar surroundings. In a rare moment alone she wandered into Prince Edward's nursery. She rarely saw Edward, his ill health kept him surrounded by governesses and nurses each assigned a task to keep the future King well and prepare him for his place on the throne. When she did see the prince, she felt uncomfortable. It reminded her that Jane Seymour had done something no other Queen had accomplished. Give the King a male heir.

She nodded to acknowledge the curtsies and chorus of "Your Majesty" as she entered the room.

"How is his health?" she asked.

"The child is feeling better," the nurse said and motioned her to come closer.

Katheryn peered at the boy from a distance. This was not her territory and she felt more comfortable remaining near the doorway. "I have heard he is not well. That he has had fevers," she said.

"Not from lack of care. He receives the best of it under our watchful eyes," said the nurse sharply.

"I didn't mean to insult you." Katheryn blushed.

The child cried and immediately a governess ran to him.

"He'll be happy for a brother. Now that Edward has reached the age of four he has no need of my breast," said the wet nurse. "Shall we be hearing the good news soon?"

Katheryn felt anything but Queenly at the moment. She looked from one to the other, but no one spoke, waiting to hear her response. "With your assistance I'm sure the King has nothing to fear. Edward will inherit the throne.

Edward may have been born a weakling, but he'll not die that way." With that, she turned and exited the room.

"They say she's barren," whispered the wet nurse after Katheryn had gone.

The women shook their heads, and tongues clicked in disapproval.

If a week passed, while on tour, without a visit from Thomas Culpeper, it was unusual. Now all the sneaking about and uncertainty had left her drained. She glanced over at Lady Rochford. She looked horrible. The strain left her thinner, more pale and nervous than even previously. Of course, she made all the arrangements but experienced only vicarious pleasure at the outcome.

Katheryn understood Lady Rochford's motivation. She saw her eyes grow narrow, her breath race, her lips become dry and need constant attention from her tongue whenever Thomas Culpeper was in their presence.

"Soon I will sit for the artist Holbein," Katheryn said. "I have been married over year, and still no portrait. The King promised that after the tour was completed I should have my opportunity. If he can do for me what he did for Anna I should be quite happy!"

"Flattering portraits are what Holbein does best," Lady Rochford said.

"It is shameful that I have none. Tomorrow we shall right that."

"And tonight?" Lady Rochford looked at Katheryn.

"Yes tonight. Bring him to me. Past midnight. Here." Lady Margaret Douglas swept into the room and silenced the exchange.

"I'll be needing a bath, Lady Margaret. Plenty of wood for the fire, as it is cold. Who knows when I shall find it warm enough again to bathe?"

"Yes, Your Majesty." Margaret backed out of the room with a bow.

The bath sat before a large fire. Katheryn felt her right shoulder burn with the heat, but her left one was chilly, exposed to the cold air. She stepped her foot into the water to test it, and then lowered her body as her ladies lifted the gown up over her head. She did not mind the act of bathing since becoming Queen. Previously she had always been cold and uncomfortable but now with two ladies in attendance and three others to do her bidding and test the water, she enjoyed the ritual.

She was not shy about undressing before them. Seeing the Queen naked gave the ladies something to talk about, and she was certain they did. Idle much of the time, they filled their days with chatter and rumor—she wondered if they shared her secrets with the gentlemen of the court. Any one of them could probably make good money. God knows there were plenty of gentlemen who would pay to hear news of her body and its hidden pleasures. But it was treasonous for them to talk that way of the Queen—so she doubted that more than just a casual slip ever passed their tongues. She lifted her hair and closed her eyes as Lady Rochford poured the warm water over her back.

"It feels good," she said and glanced down at her belly imagining it rounded and carrying a child.

The last time Thomas laid with her they placed both their hands on the exact spot and rubbed it, dreaming of the baby they would have. "It must look like you because then it will be as handsome as the sun," Katheryn said.

"But not so much the King will see it," Thomas answered.

Katheryn closed her eyes and imagined holding the baby up to Thomas and the joy in his eyes when he took it into his arms. She managed to erase the King completely from her dreams, and drifted further and further from reality every time she conjured up the image.

"Your Majesty?" Lady Margaret interrupted her reverie.

Katheryn opened her eyes and glanced up at the servants leaning over her with curious expressions. She felt a jump in her chest as she wondered whether she had been daydreaming aloud.

Katheryn moved her nervous fingers through her hair to draw attention away from herself. "My hair is awful. Wash and comb it. I can't remember the last time it was done properly." She pouted and sank deeper into the tub. "I'm cold."

She noticed lately she had been feeling angrier and angrier each time that she was pulled away from her fantasies and back into her surroundings.

Lady Rochford tugged at her hair and then threw a pitcher of water upon it. Katheryn squealed.

"Stop, Lady Rochford. You are hurting me!" She slid down into the water until her hair, and most of her face, was submerged. When she opened her eyes she saw Lady Rochford leaning over her, and she wondered if she meant to drown her.

Having waited up most of the night, expecting a visit or at least a word from Thomas Culpeper, Katheryn could no longer float peacefully away into her daydreams to pass the time. Fearful that some harm had befallen him, she could not sleep. It had to be well past midnight. Lady Rochford had disappeared and brought her no news. Her ears detected nothing. She sat on the edge of the bed and dangled her feet toward the floor. "It is a prison. In Lambeth I could go where I wanted. I was free and happy."

She jumped to her feet and practiced a dance step, holding her nightgown from her body she swayed and turned aimlessly. For a moment it entered her mind that perhaps Thomas had tired of her, and meant never to be alone with her again. Never to love her again. Her feet stopped and suddenly she felt a cold chill and noticed the temperature of the room against her skin. Never again to feel his body and his breath. To know only the bloated, smelly body of the King for the rest of her life.

She grabbed her head and clutched it in both her hands, pulling it downward by the long tresses. "It's a prison!" she said loudly. "I am going mad!"

She raced around the room and flung herself, belly first, upon the bed. "If I have to live without him I will throw myself from the window. I swear I would do it." Her words muffled into the bed covers. "I swear I will."

# CHAPTER 21

The next morning, sleep having arrived at four o'clock, and then only fitfully, Katheryn was in no mood for the cheerful ministrations of her staff. She glanced at Lady Rochford angrily; it was her fault that Thomas Culpeper never arrived last night. She was unable to question her until they could be alone, and Lady Rochford's blank expression infuriated her.

"Today in a special service of Thanksgiving the King will say his prayers in honor of Queen Katheryn. All the churches in all the land will be required to do the same. His most *virtuous* Queen." Katheryn was certain she was being mocked.

"Not so virtuous as you, Lady Rochford," she said sharply.

The others glanced at Lady Rochford, certain that the exchange had meaning. But what? Margaret Douglas placed her hand on Katheryn's shoulder. "We shall make you shine today."

Katheryn saw her reflection—the crease on her cheek, the worry-line between her brows. "For what purpose?" she asked.

"Why to please the King, of course," said Margaret.

"Oh yes, to please the King."

"We must hurry," said Lady Rochford.

"Do what you will with me, I am without strength today."

Being in the Chapel Royal annoyed Katheryn. She agreed that it was beautiful with its ornate ceiling. The brilliant blue color contrasted sharply with gold and red accents, and Katheryn had always admired the cherubs hanging gracefully high above her head. It wasn't the chapel itself that annoyed Katheryn; it was the fact that the King always seemed so at home and happy to be there.

Katheryn was certain he felt even more powerful in this place, surrounded by the reminder that he was second only to God.

Her ears detected the words, "...Thou hast been pleased to give me a wife..." and she wondered where she heard those words before. Oh yes, at his bed when he thought her asleep. She still didn't know what happened to Culpeper and her anger at Lady Rochford had only increased with the passing time.

Suddenly her eyes caught a movement at the back of the chapel—Archbishop Cranmer. Why was he not seated, she wondered? As he came closer she noticed a letter in his hands—she also noticed that although her eyes were upon him, his eyes were doing everything possible to avoid her. Silently, he placed the letter at the King's side, nodded his head, bowed and swept out of the chapel as quickly as he had arrived.

Something about his manner reminded Katheryn of the day Henry Mannox placed a letter in the Duchess' pew. Her throat tightened. Henry took little notice of the Archbishop, but focused upon Katheryn, his smile broad and childlike. Cranmer paused at the door and turned to view the King as he doted upon his beautiful wife. Katheryn thought she detected something different about the Archbishop. He looked even more of a sourpuss than usual.

Henry waved the letter at Cranmer. Cranmer flinched, expecting a spittle of rage to spew forth. Instead a laugh, deep and hearty, emerged. "My Lord?"

"Rumors and idle gossip. We must protect the Queen from the malicious and evil heathens who wish to destroy her. Thank you, Cranmer, for bringing this to my attention. My opinion of Queen Katheryn remains constant. I intend to send William Fitzwilliam, the Earl of Southampton and the Lord Privy Seal to London to re-examine both John Lascelles and his sister Mary. They shall cough up the truth and an end will be put to these lies."

Henry threw the letter upon the table and then his arm about the Archbishop's shoulders. "Did you hear my prayer of Thanksgiving yesterday?" he said.

"Yes, My Lord," said the Archbishop.

"Be careful. She is my only love," Henry whispered in his ear.

Mary Lascelles' brother, John, sat nervously upon the wooden bench and stared up at the three men surrounding him. His bug-eyes didn't move behind the quickly fluttering lids. His lips were dry, and he licked them furiously. "My sister does not lie," he said once again.

"We can have you tortured," said the Earl of Southampton.

"And still I would tell you my sister is not a liar. If she says the Queen was not a maid upon her marriage to the King then I will trust she speaks the truth."

Fitzwilliam pulled a knife and placed it underneath his chin. "I you are lying you will die a most painful death."

John Lascelles swallowed and blinked—he dared not move, fearful of the knife's edge—but his eyes did not stray from the gentlemen before him.

"I believe him," Fitzwilliam said and withdrew the knife.

John rubbed his hands back and forth beneath his chin. "Question my sister if you will. She knew the Queen before her appointment to the Royal Court. My sister does not lie."

"They lie!" screamed Henry.

Cranmer now had reason to flinch against the King. "Both Mary and John Lascelles have been questioned and they swear to the accuracy of their story, My Lord. It is painful for me to tell you that it has come to my attention that Sir Francis Derehem has recently been employed by the Queen as her personal secretary."

Henry's chest deflated and his arm stopped mid-motion. "What?" he asked quietly.

"The truth," said Cranmer.

Henry fell into his chair. "Round them up. All of them. Do what you must to gain the truth. Spare nothing. Katheryn is to be locked in her chambers."

His raspy breath filled the room and he put his head in his hands and turned his eyes away. Cranmer did not move.

"Be gone!" said the King suddenly. "I should find great pleasure in putting you upon the rack with them. If my eyes see you again today, I will call you a traitor as well!"

# CHAPTER 22

Henry Mannox sat upon a chair, hands bound before him. What crime had he committed? He was imprisoned in the Tower of London and seated before Sir Thomas Wriothesley who had rounded him up and dragged him here.

Mannox knew well the type of torture instruments housed in the Tower and he was certain that there were others he had never heard of.

"I have no quarrel with you myself, Master Mannox," said Thomas Wriothesley. "It is your past relationship with the Queen that the King and his Council are interested in."

Henry blinked and wet his lips. "Might I have something to drink as my mouth is parched," Henry said.

"Certainly." Thomas signaled to the guard to fetch some ale. "It is true that the Duchess hired you to instruct the Queen upon the virginal?"

"Yes, sir." Henry licked his lips again, and glanced toward the door hoping for the guard's return.

"And you were intimate with her?" Thomas raised his eyebrows and smiled falsely to encourage a reply.

"I have committed no crime, sir. It is true that I commonly used to feel the secrets and other parts of the Queen's body. She allowed it."

Henry, unable to reach with his hands for the ale now being offered by the guard, parted his lips to receive the liquid. A bit of it spilled over and ran down his chin onto his legs. No one offered to wipe it away.

"You knew her carnally?" said his inquisitor.

"She was a maid when she left me. I did not have her maidenhead. It was Sir Francis Derehem took that from her—and from the King. I swear she was young and I left her intact."

"I believe you," Sir Thomas said. "I cannot answer for the King."

"It is you I blame for this last mischief!" Henry waved his finger toward his assembled Council members. "I have none other to blame for this succession of such ill-conditioned wives!" No one dared to look at him. The Duke of Norfolk stared at his hands, Archbishop Cranmer and Sir Thomas Writhosley at the floor. They knew that Henry's rage was just beginning its grand assent before exploding. Cromwell was killed for less. Henry moved between them, his large body thrust them apart as it brushed by.
"You!" He grabbed the Duke by the cloak. "The Howards shall pay for this."
"I had no knowledge!" said the Duke.
"All shall be questioned. Upon the rack if necessary. Torture them until they tell me the truth!" He circled the room striking out randomly at whoever happened to be in his way. "Bring me my sword! I shall go slay her myself! I shall slay her that I loved so much!" He moved wildly, searching the room. "That wicked woman shall know the full measure of pain she has caused me. Torture!" he screamed and stopped, frozen in place.
The sudden silence lifted the gaze of his Council. Henry's head was thrown backward and his eyes were glazed over and fuzzy. His large body swayed and bucked as though it might topple and a gurgle rose from his chest and exploded from his mouth.
His hands covered his face and he stumbled to his chair and collapsed with a sob. Cranmer looked at the Duke. Henry's massive body shook and writhed and he gasped for air and rocked the room with his cries. No one dared to move, uncertain of what path to take. This amount of pain and sorrow they had never before witnessed from their King. They had seen doubt, grief, anger, joy, even some tears, but never such a total collapse.
Cranmer leaned over to the Duke and whispered, "I fear he has gone mad." The Duke nodded his head in agreement.

Queen Katheryn swung Francis Derehem playfully about the floor as her ladies watched. Lady Margaret and Lady Rochford clasped hands and joined in; practicing the new steps Katheryn had taught them. Earlier that morning the Queen's mood had lifted when Lady Rochford informed her that Culpeper had merely gone a-hawking and should return in a few days. Lady Rochford, out of breath, pulled away from her partner and stood by the door to watch Francis and the Queen.

"He is in love with her, you know," she whispered to Katherine Tylney after she sidled up next to her. "But not so in love with the Queen as some others."

Katherine Tylney raised her eyebrows hoping to encourage the release of additional information. Lady Rochford winked but kept her lips tightly pursed.

Tired from the gaiety, Katheryn threw herself upon the stool of her dressing table and lifted her skirt to cool her legs. Francis fanned her neck with the back of his hand.

"The duties of personal secretary have been much expanded since Francis Derehem acquired the post," said Katherine Tylney.

"Indeed."

The Queen leaned backward and smiled up at Francis, revealing her neck and cleavage. "Dear Francis, cool my face," she said and grabbed his hand to pull it back and forth across her cheek.

Obligingly, he let it graze her lips with wispy light strokes, just delicate enough to appear accidental. Katheryn's eyes closed and she parted her lips to allow the full indulgence of the experience.

Lady Rochford turned her head at the sound of footsteps in the hall and leaned out to see who was approaching. Archbishop Cranmer and the Duke of Norfolk were flanked by four of the King's guards. Their solemn faces drew the color from Lady Rochford's cheeks and caused her heart to race.

She ran to the Queen and Francis. "Quickly," she said. She thrust Francis to the floor. He protested and pushed her away.

"Quiet," Lady Rochford said. "It will not go well for you if you are found here." Lady Rochford lifted Katheryn's skirt and indicated to Francis to crawl underneath. No sooner was Francis huddled between the Queen's legs then a white and shaking Duke burst in on them.

"You are a whore, Katheryn! You have been a whore since the day you were born, and you shall die a whore!" A stern Cranmer stepped in front of the Duke and signaled him to be silent.

The ladies huddled in a corner, and Lady Rochford, weaker and paler than any of them, braced herself upon the dressing table.

"What is the meaning of this?" said Katheryn, unable to rise and confront her accusers due to the gentleman beneath her skirt. "How dare you call me a whore! I am the Queen! You bow to me! You serve me!" Her legs shook, her face flared with anger, her body twisted from the waist, as best it could, to look at them.

Cranmer took a step toward her. "There will be no more time for dancing. No more time for merry-making," he stated flatly. "The ladies shall come with me and you are to be locked in your chambers."

The Duke walked to Katheryn and leaned over so that his mouth was inches from her ear and his face reflected in the mirror next to hers. "I shan't be taken down with you, dear niece. I escaped the downfall of Anne Boleyn, the 'Great Whore,' and I shall escape your downfall as well. 'The Greatest Whore.'"

He lifted her to standing—he was strong enough to pull her, even against her will. He glanced down at Francis Derehem's foot protruding beneath the Queen's skirt. The Duke raised the dress higher to reveal the quaking mass at his feet.

"What have we here?" He signaled to Cranmer and the guards to draw closer. Francis lifted his head and terrified eyes to the men.

"All in this room are considered guilty of treason," said the Duke.

"It is rather suspicious," said the Archbishop.

"It was Lady Rochford's idea!" said Katheryn.

"The Queen is guilty!" said Lady Rochford.

"We shall get to the bottom of this," Cranmer said.

"Take them away!" said the Duke, "and guard her room. We shall return."

Francis' eyes wouldn't clear. He blinked over and over, but the blows to his head had muddied his vision. His bare cheek pressed into cold, damp stone. His nose detected the odor of burning flesh. Or was it? How long had he been here, he wondered? He shuddered when a memory flashed through his mind. The question: "Have you known the Queen carnally?" was the last thing he remembered.

# CHAPTER 23

Katheryn's body shook ferociously. Like cold fingers, fear traveled up and down her spine and set her limbs trembling. When the shaking reached its most powerful moment and set her entire body into spasm—it subsided, leaving her frozen until the tremor began again, a tiny movement at the base of her spine ready to travel in waves until it overtook her completely.

As the light faded and no one returned for her, the loneliness overwhelmed her until she began to pace back-and-forth, up-and-down the floor. When she felt herself on the brink of madness, she would steel herself by thinking of an action, any action she might perform to extricate herself from this dilemma.

What do they know? What has Lady Rochford told them? What will be done to me? Over and over these thoughts were repeated, sometimes spoken aloud, sometimes merely bleeding into her consciousness before being replaced by the next thought.

The trembling began again, but not enough to obscure the question, "What have they done to Francis?" Nor the image of him stretched upon the rack. It was more than she could tolerate and she threw herself upon the bed and clutched her head to obliterate the thought.

All night long she alternated between endless pacing and desperately throwing her body onto the bed as tears began to flow. Morning light found her pacing the room once again. A new thought had entered her mind. "I must see the King. I must see the King." She chanted as she walked.

Her face was swollen; tiny purple dots had exploded around her eyes from the force of her anguish. The night had transformed her from a beautiful, young Queen into a trapped animal.

The door to her chambers opened at last, and she lifted her eyes and stared wildly at the two guards as they entered the room. She noticed the shocked look upon their faces as they stared back at her.

Katheryn smoothed her hair with her hands. "I am feeling quite well now. Might I have something to drink?" She motioned across the room at her dressing table. "Please bring me a comb as well." The guards bowed and turned away to perform the tasks requested of them.

Katheryn eyed the open door. Quick as a fox she was on her feet and outside before either guard noticed her departure. In fact, it was her voice that spun them about and made them aware of the missing prisoner.

Her body charged down the hall toward the King's chapel. Her cries echoed off the walls. "My Lord!" she screamed, certain that he was performing morning prayers.

"Save me! My God! Save me! I am a miserable wretch! My husband, my King, my savior!" She let a wail erupt and continue unending until the last breath had been choked from her body.

The Duke and Archbishop Cranmer stepped in front of her. Each one grabbed an arm. She fell between them and they lifted her body off the floor. But the fight had not gone out of her. With a last burst of energy she twisted her upper body against their tightening grasp. No words, just sounds exploded from her now.

Like a wild beast with its leg caught in a trap she twisted round and round to free herself. The action caused their fingers to dig into her arms as metal digs deeper and deeper into an animal's wound. She was certain Henry would fling open the door and rescue her. He must. He could not resist her. He told her himself.

Inside the Chapel, Henry's head was bowed in prayer. He had spent much of the night that way. No one dared bother him. In and out of his numbed state thoughts bled as well. For him the thoughts were of God and Katheryn.

His faith in both was so badly shaken that his shoulders bent heavily with the weight of his defeat.

What he feared most, the thought that shook him to the core and sent the trembling through his body, was the one that perhaps God was punishing him. Perhaps, I have not done right by God. He could not allow himself to journey all the way back to his first wife. He must have been acting on God's wishes when he divorced her. He must have been acting on God's wishes when he divorced himself from the Pope. And it was God's wish that those who wronged against him be punished. Her beauty muddled my brain. How many others had it muddled? She brought her lover into court as her personal secretary.

He sobbed, letting the tears land on his folded hands and then roll onto the floor. He stared at his hands. How fat they were. He looked at them closely, inspecting the creases and folds. As a young man his hands were strong and sure. He was feared and admired. Now he was laughed at. Everyone must have known that his wife was taking lovers behind his back. The cuckold fat man. From great Prince to buffoon.

A roar escaped his throat. He lifted his face to the ceiling and bellowed once again. They would pay! All of them. Any person that had known of this and laughed at him behind his back would be drawn and quartered. Burned. Stretched upon the rack. Blinded, mutilated, destroyed. They would not laugh anymore. The King and God would laugh last.

A cry. In the hall. He turned his head toward the sound.

"My Lord! Help me!" A scream.

His heart stopped in his chest then rushed onward like a drumbeat. More screams. He knew the voice. His body rose and in a daze he walked toward the sound. He stopped. His feet planted firmly. He lifted his hands once more and inspected them. "A fat buffoon no more," he whispered.

Another scream. He pressed his hands to his ears. "Stop!" he yelled. "Stop it!" He raced from the sound, his aching legs stumbling down the aisle toward the altar. "Stop. I will not save you, Katheryn. I cannot save you! I cannot save you!"


"You were precontracted in marriage to Francis Derehem?" said Archbishop Cranmer.

"No, sir."

"He has told us of the precontract. He admits he laid with you as husband and wife, but swears that there was a precontract."

"No, sir."

Katheryn is dazed, thought the Archbishop. Just look at her. She focuses everywhere but into my face. She is distant and confused.

"Do you understand what is being said?" he said politely.

"Yes, sir."

"You were considering marriage to Francis Derehem when you laid with him in carnal union." He wanted to clarify the matter.

"I could not marry Francis Derehem. I am a Howard. It would not be allowed. It is below my station to marry Francis Derehem." Katheryn smiled politely and ran her hands back and forth through her hair.

"I am a vile wretch. Unworthy to be called either wife or subject to the King. You tell him that I have said this. You tell him that I am his most humble servant and beg him for mercy. Tell him that I understand that he is a man of infinite goodness and piety and that I am a disgraceful wretch unworthy to look upon him, and too vile to expect mercy, but please ask him for mercy, kind sir. You will tell him?" She raised her eyebrows hopefully and when Cranmer leaned closer to hear the soft words, she reached out her hand to stroke his cheek, like a mother to a child.

Cranmer cleared his throat, uncomfortable with this response. She was doing nothing that he expected of her.

"Do you understand that a precontract will annul the marriage to the King and may save your life?" said Cranmer.

"Yes, sir. How can a Howard marry below her station? My uncle the Duke would never allow it." She looked at him as though he were a child and too stupid to understand the meaning of her words. She let go a tittering laugh.

Cranmer stood and paced the room. "Katheryn, the King will not see you. He is leaving today. He will not be here for me to deliver your message."

Katheryn jumped to her feet and raced over to him. "What have you said?"

"The King has left Hampton Court. He will not be available for petition. You must deal with me and the Council."

Katheryn raised her hand and struck him soundly about the face. Not once, but two, three times before he grabbed her hand and held her tightly. She brought her teeth down upon his wrist and he screamed and jumped away, shaking the injury wildly in the air.

"Unhand me! I am Queen. I am the Queen. I must see my husband. The King. My husband is King of England. Have you forgotten? You are my servant not my ruler. Bring me my King. I will answer to him only!"

She raced about the room, rushing at the door that Cranmer had locked behind him. "Give me the key. You can not hold me here!"

Cranmer was unmoved, and she stopped and looked up into his stony eyes. For half a minute they stood still and looked at one another to see who would flinch first. Katheryn's breath drew heavily but Cranmer barely breathed.

"It's over, Katheryn. Unless you tell us the truth," he said quietly.

The shaking began again. From the base of her spine it rose like a fountain, forcing her to go limp. Another wail released from her chest and she threw herself upon the bed and rocked side-to-side. Cranmer watched her for a moment then shook his head sorrowfully. Without a goodbye he put the key into the door and let himself out.

# CHAPTER 24

Six French hoods, six pairs of sleeves and six gowns, accompanied the Queen to her quarters in the former Abbey of Syon at Brentford in Middlesex where she was to sit under house arrest. Katheryn remembered that the Abbey was where the King's niece, Margaret Douglas, had been sent for falling in love with Katheryn's brother without the King's consent. She also remembered that Margaret had been released from the Abbey after the King felt she had learned her lesson. It gave Katheryn hope that she had been placed here and not in the Tower of London.

On the King's orders all of Katheryn's clothes were to be without jewels and all of her ladies were to be above reproach.

Lady Rochford sat in the Tower to await questioning. Her character and role in this matter were under interrogation. She rubbed her cold hands together and eyed the door, waiting for the moment when she would be given the chance to declare her innocence. Three days she sat with only a brief interchange with the guard as food and drink were slipped to her.

Currently the Council was questioning Katherine Tylney. Sir Thomas Wriothesley asked about the Queen's behavior on the northern progress. "Well," he said, "did you notice any strange goings-on with the Queen? Had she left her bedchamber at any time?"

Mrs. Tylney eyed the Council members. Their blank stares caused her to swallow and stammer. "Yes sir, I did indeed. You see while in Lincoln the Queen left her room on two occasions and went to Lady Rochford's chamber, which was up two short flights of stairs. I remember that she sent the ladies away—but by two o'clock she had still not come to bed. The second night I was forced to wait outside Lady Rochford's bedroom. I do not know what went on inside. I swear sirs, I do not know. However, I might add, that I am certain she went to Lady Rochford's chamber to meet with someone."

Wriothesley smacked his lips and brought his fist down upon the table. He was pleased with this information, no matter how vague. He motioned to the other Council members as if to say, see I knew it.

"I have no further knowledge," Katherine said.

"Thank you, Mrs. Tylney. If your services are required in the future you will be informed." Wriothesley waved her away.

Katherine flushed and stood with a bow. She could not say anymore, for a catch had come into her throat. She realized that her testimony may mean grave harm to the Queen and she wanted nothing more than to be gone.

When the door closed behind her, Wriothesley reiterated what he had heard. "Derehem went to meet his lover, the Queen. It is obvious that Lady Rochford had a hand in it as well. It seems perfectly evident to me."

"We need more proof," said Cranmer. "Call in Margaret Morton. She was in service to the Queen during the progress, perhaps she can add to this."

The room was grim when Margaret Morton entered. Nobody liked Margaret Morton much. The Council knew her nature. She was a gossip. For that reason she was useful to them. Although she had no notion of what others had told the Council, she knew that whatever it was it couldn't be good for the Queen. Motioned to sit, she did so, nodding one at a time to the gentlemen before her.

"I am told," she began without a question having gone her way, "that the Council is interested in the affairs of the Queen. I have reason to believe her guilt—at Lincoln, Pontefract and York she acted peculiar. I remember at Pontefract she had angry words with myself and Mrs. Luffkyn, another chamberer. We were forbidden to assist her or even enter her bedchamber. I know for a fact that Lady Rochford delivered letters between the Queen and another. I had always assumed the other was Thomas Culpeper."

Margaret paused for a breath; she enjoyed holding center stage. At the mention of Thomas Culpeper she noticed a startled look on the face of each Council member. It dawned on her that she had provided them with new information. She smiled gleefully.

"Gentlemen, I would swear by the look upon your faces I have given a name new to your ears. I never mistrusted the Queen until at Hatfield I saw her look out of her chamber window on Master Culpeper, after such a sort that I thought there was love between them." She paused to let the Council feel the full impact of her words then leaned forward as another thought entered her mind. "Once when Katheryn had been alone with Culpeper for five or six hours I was certain by the noises they made that they had passed out." She winked to seal her meaning.

"Passed out?" questioned Archbishop Cranmer.

Norfolk interrupted the Archbishop. "We understand the term." He whispered to Cranmer that indeed the lady had meant the sounds of orgasm.

"You might recover a letter from the Queen to Master Culpeper. One delivered by Lady Rochford," added Margaret Morton. "It would strengthen your case."

"And why have we not heard of this before?" asked Cranmer.

"Sir, if you had suspected the Queen of adultery with the King's favorite man would you be the one to tell him? Especially if you were merely a chamberer such as myself?"

"I understand."

"It relieves me greatly to at last unburden my heavy heart. I have been weighed down by my knowledge," she added.

"It appears that many others have likewise been burdened," said Wriothesley.

"That will be all," said Archbishop Cranmer. "I am about to *pass-out* from all this new information." He said this while looking directly at Margaret Morton. She blushed deeply at the realization she had offended him. The Duke of Norfolk grinned at the humor.

She curtsied quickly and rushed ahead of the guards.

"We must call Lady Rochford. All fingers point to her. She is guilty of treason and if this is so, the King will be harsh," said Norfolk.

"Tomorrow. Tonight I need to rest," said the Archbishop and wiped his red and runny eyes with his cold chapped fingers. "Tomorrow Lady Rochford will speak."

Lady Rochford blinked her eyes at the harsh light. The Tower was dark and she hadn't seen daylight for many days. The guards held her arms tightly, but she assured them there was no need. "I speak gladly to the Council. For it is there I shall declare my innocence and be known for the loyal subject I am." The grip loosened only slightly.

She entered the council room with her chin high and her neck and back erect. She sat on the edge of her chair and folded her hands in her lap. "I offer myself willingly," she said. She smiled at Norfolk hoping to win some favor, but he showed no response.

"It is my niece's relationship with both Francis Derehem and Thomas Culpeper we are interested in," said Norfolk.

"I have no knowledge of the Queen's relationship with Francis Derehem. He may have loved her, but she used his affections to make Thomas Culpeper jealous—nothing more. Thomas and Queen Katheryn would argue fiercely at times and I heard her say he had best beware for there was, behind the door, another."

"Meaning?" said the Archbishop.

"Meaning another lover," she replied. "At first Thomas Culpeper showed his affections to the Queen and she rebuked him. Culpeper persisted and eventually as you can see he won her affections."

The Council was speechless. This amount of information shocked them. Argued fiercely? Jealous of Francis Derehem? Culpeper and Katheryn lovers for so much time? It seemed to them that it was only the Council and the King who had no knowledge of the Queen's misdeeds.

"Lady Rochford. It has been made clear to us by other accounts that you knew of this affair and that you aided and abetted it," said Wriothesley.

"I was forced by the Queen to arrange their meetings against my will. I swear it. I knew nothing of sexual intercourse between them. Although I do not doubt that it occurred. I am an innocent party to this madness—I merely obeyed the orders of my Mistress. Nothing more.

Her evil doings should not rub off on me." Lady Rochford was agitated now; certain that they meant to accuse her of treason.

"I am unconvinced," said Archbishop Cranmer.

"I too have my doubts," Norfolk said.

"The King shall decide your punishment," said Wriothesley. "Take her away for now. We shall see you again, Lady Rochford. You can count on it."

Lady Rochford trembled as she was lifted from her chair. "Please, sirs. I am an innocent party. You must believe me."

"There are few innocents in this sad and treasonous tale," said Cranmer.

Lady Rochford reeled forward; she did not fall to the floor, for the guards caught her.

Syon was comfortable and Katheryn retained the use of four ladies-in-waiting and twelve servants. It eased her mind that the King had been lenient with her and placed her in so generous a surrounding even if she was without any cloth of estate or sumptuous gowns. Her servants were friendly enough—cordial, aloof mostly—still uncertain as to the full nature of Katheryn's crimes.

The first attempt to wring a confession out of Katheryn had proven unsuccessful. This time both Archbishop Cranmer and Sir Thomas Wriothesley meant to get what they needed. When they arrived at Syon they found Katheryn in good spirits, with needlepoint in her hands, ringed by her servants. She entertained them with a story.

When she saw Cranmer, she stopped mid-sentence. He brushed away the women with a wave of his hand and closed the door behind them.

"Katheryn," he said. "We know of your meetings with Thomas Culpeper."

Her face became ashen and Cranmer, concerned that she would once again become hysterical and strike out at him, touched her shoulder. "Do not flail about this time, it will do you no good."

Katheryn blinked, swallowed and laid the needlepoint upon the floor. "Oh, that little, sweet fool. I presented him with a cap and a ring, but he means nothing to me."

Wriothesley grabbed her shoulder harshly and gave her a shake. "Wake up. We are not stupid. We know everything that transpired between you."

Cranmer lifted a paper to her face. "This is a full confession of your misdeeds. We require your signature upon it."

Her eyes lifted slowly toward the paper. Wriothesley walked to the writing table to procure a pen to assist her.

"I cannot sign this," she said.

"You have not read it."

"I will not lay my hand to lies drafted by the Council."

"Lies? Is that what you call them? We have witnesses."

"Witnesses to what?" said Katheryn.

"To your adulterous misdeeds. Lady Rochford tells us that you were in her chambers from eleven o'clock in the evening to four o'clock in the morning. Mrs. Tylney has confirmed it. They say you went to meet with…"

Wriothesley stopped, hoping she would say the name. She looked at him but said nothing.

"Thomas Culpeper," said the Archbishop.

"I tell you, Thomas Culpeper's nothing more to me than a sweet fool. He fancied me."

Wriothesley walked behind Katheryn. He grabbed her by the throat and pulled her head backward.

"Your uncle, the Duke, has been talking very ill of you. He says you prostituted yourself with six, seven, eight lovers. He calls you 'The Greatest Whore!' Your confession says nothing of the others. We are kind to you it seems."

"My uncle has the heart of a snake. He knows nothing of my affairs, real or imagined. He lies to save himself. He distances himself from his niece to save his neck. He thought well enough of me to propose marriage to the King."

Cranmer pulled Wriothesley's hand off Katheryn and pushed the paper at her once more. "Sign it, Katheryn. A full confession of carnal knowledge with Thomas Culpeper and Francis Derehem."

Katheryn's eyes closed. She sat motionless, her bosom lifted rapidly with each breath. "I deny upon oath any carnal knowledge of Master Culpeper. I begged Lady Rochford to leave me alone, but she insisted that I meet with him. Indeed he was full in love with me, but I rebuked his affections. I swear this is so."

Cranmer looked at her tear-filled eyes and pained face and felt genuine sorrow. "Would you be certain that Culpeper would report the same story, even under torture?" he said.

Katheryn jumped up and clutched onto his body. "Please do not torture him. Spare him. Please. He will tell you the truth. Force will not be necessary. I swear it. Do not harm him." Cranmer glanced at Wriothesley who raised his eyebrows at him.

"Please sir, he is a nobleman."

Wriothesley pushed her away. "I have found nothing noble in his behavior. Or the Queen's." He motioned to Cranmer to exit. As he left, Cranmer glanced backward into the room. Katheryn stood, her trembling hands crossed at her stomach, her head bowed low; a child frightened by the thought of the beating she was soon to receive.

# CHAPTER 25

December 1st, 1541 saw the trial of Culpeper and Derehem. They sat side-by-side before the Privy Council. The room was crowded with faces they didn't recognize. Foreign ambassadors had come to witness that these men, accused of high treason, were being treated fairly; but it added to the carnival environment.

Francis remembered when he had participated in the game of bear-baiting. The bear, tied to a rope, was tortured and besieged by hounds until exhausted. It was sport. Well, he thought, today he and Culpeper were the bears and these men were the hounds ripping at their throats.

"Francis Derehem, you are brought before this Council on charges of presumptive treason. Queen Katheryn Howard is believed to have lived an abominable, base, carnal, voluptuous, and licentious life as befits a common harlot, while maintaining an appearance of chastity and honesty. She let the King fall in love with her, believing she was pure, and she arrogantly contracted and coupled herself in marriage although it is now known she was a harlot before and an adulteress after. This Council has reason to believe that you were pre-contracted in marriage and had carnal knowledge of the Queen and yet you allowed her marriage to proceed illegally. You also continued your relationship and knew her carnally after her marriage. How do you plead?"

Francis glanced over at Culpeper. Although they never liked one another, they were now soulmates, joined by their experiences with, and love for, one woman.

"Not guilty," said Derehem clearly. He swallowed and choked on his saliva causing a coughing spell that interrupted the court for almost a minute.

"Well," said the Archbishop. "It seems those words have caught in your throat." Francis squirmed uncomfortably in his seat.

"Thomas Culpeper," said the Privy Seal. "You are accused of criminal intercourse with the Queen on August 29, 1541 at Pontefract and at other times. You are accused of inciting the Queen to adultery. Queen Katheryn confessed to loving you above the King and all others. How do you plead?"

"Not guilty." Thomas Culpeper did not look him in the eye.

"*Not* guilty?" said the Archbishop.

"Not guilty," he said again.


The Duchess was puzzled. Her servant, Pewson, had broken the news that the Queen was under arrest for adultery. "With Francis Derehem," he said.

Her wrinkled face looked at him in wonder. "Adultery? What do you mean?"

"She has played the King false. The rumors are spreading that soon all Howards shall be arrested and questioned."

She stared at him blankly. She did not comprehend the full impact of his meaning. "Arrested? The Howards?"

"Questioned about Queen Katheryn. They say she was precontracted to Francis Derehem and knew him as husband before her marriage to the King. And after."

The Duchess rose from her chair and shuffled about the room before she answered. "We must protect ourselves. Bring me any papers and effects of Master Derehem's. Anything in this household to which he had laid claim must be destroyed."

"Yes, Your Grace." Pewson bowed and left her alone.

"Can this be true? What fault can they find with me? I am certainly blameless. If what Pewson says is true, then Katheryn and her lover deserve to be hanged." Pewson entered the room with Derehem's coffer.

"Lay it here," said the Duchess and pointed to her writing table. "I will peruse the contents at my leisure." She waved him away.

Left alone, she opened the box and withdrew papers and trinkets. Her feeble hands spread the papers open, but her eyes had trouble with the words and she squinted and lifted the document away from her face. "I shall burn them. Any signs of familiarity with Master Derehem must be destroyed." She placed the objects back into the wooden box and carried it to the fire. The flames had died a bit and she stirred them with her cane before throwing everything on top.

A knock on the door announced the arrival of her servant William Ashby. "Yes?" she said coldly.

"The Duke of Norfolk, Your Grace."

"Send him in. William?" she asked. "Would you say that I was familiar with Francis Derehem?"

"Familiar?"

"That I had knowledge of his affairs."

"Affairs?"

"His comings-and-goings. His women and such."

"You and Master Derehem have been friendly for some time, Your Grace."

"Speak no more of it. Send in the Duke."

"Yes, Your Grace."

When the Duke entered, he found the Duchess in her chair looking pale and weak.

"Your Grace," he said with a bow. "You are not well?"

"Not at all. I have been quite ill and am going to take to my bed. I do not know how long I shall be bedridden." She smiled weakly at him.

"I have come at the request of the Privy Council to bring you for questioning."

"Questioning? Whatever for?"

"Surely you must have received news of Queen Katheryn's predicament."

"How could the affairs of an adulteress Queen possibly be of concern to me?"

"We have reason to believe you had knowledge of the precontract between Francis Derehem and Katheryn."

"Precontract? It is the first I have heard of such a thing. Please send for my servant, I must go to bed." She toppled over in her chair and began to shake. "I am quite ill you see."

The Duke noticed the large wooden coffer smoking in the fire behind her. He walked to it and knelt to get a closer look. "You have been busy burning papers. Francis Derehem's perhaps. I suspect so." He reached in to retrieve an unburnt bit of parchment. "Your illness will not save you. The Council is certain to order your arrest, if necessary."

"Leave me. I am an old and ill woman. Let your Council come to me with their questions, they will learn nothing."

"As you wish." The Duke bowed and exited without a goodbye.

The flesh on Francis Derehem's back burnt with the first stroke of the whip. He knew that there was only worse to follow. He turned his face away but was felled by the next stroke.

The Duke of Norfolk raised his hand to signal the dungeon-keeper to cease the whip. He leaned over Francis and breathed into his ear. "It is illegal to use torture to wring a confession from a prisoner. Unless, of course, the crime is treason and the King has ordered it. Then it is as if the law had never been written. We used the brakes to force out all of your friend Damport's teeth, for no other reason, than he knew you well. He spoke. You shall confess your guilt before the day is through."

"I have never had criminal intercourse with the Queen. I have confessed to knowing her prior to her marriage, but I swear to you never afterwards." Derehem shook uncontrollably, his fear finally overtook him and he felt his eyes fill with tears. "For the love of God, this is your niece. You have been her greatest champion. How can you abandon her now?"

"That common harlot is no longer my relation. I have distanced myself from her heinous crimes. Do not waste your breath on me. I will not save you. Nor will I dirty my hands. There are others better suited to the job of tightening the rack. I leave them to it. When a confession has been rung from you they may rest from their weary job." He signaled to the dungeon-keeper to continue with his work. The sound of a whip punctuated his exit.

"I am guilty!" screamed Thomas Culpeper. "Guilty of harboring lustful thoughts!" These words were the last he spoke before blackness greeted him. When he once again opened his eyes he had no memory of what landed him in this cold, dark place. The feeling ebbed into his limbs and a shooting pain seared from his shoulder into his neck and head so that blackness threatened to overtake him once more.

A strange moan pierced the silence, but he felt he could no more respond to it than hope to ever stand on his own again. The moan became weak and rattled, and Thomas wondered if it were his own breath rising from his chest.

"Culpeper?" He heard someone speak his name.

"It is Francis. Culpeper?" Francis dragged his body closer to see if indeed it was Thomas lying with him. "My, God."

Thomas' left arm appeared broken in half. Two deep gashes marked his right cheek. His hair was matted with blood and his eyes were swollen shut. Francis feared they had done worse to Thomas than to himself. He reached his hand out to comfort him, but fear stopped him. Any touch might cause the poor man to suffer even more.

"Culpeper." Thomas opened his swollen eyes just enough to see the face of Derehem inches from his own. Francis tried to smile bravely at Thomas and he lay his body down next to him so that his hand lightly touched Thomas'.

They lay for about an hour that way with no words between them. At last Francis spoke. "Culpeper?" he asked. "Was she worth it?"

# CHAPTER 26

The buck charged Henry. Its eyes were wild with fear and anger, but its will refused to be broken. The wound in its side gaped and blood ran upon the ground, but its legs would not buckle. Henry raised his spear, ready for another blow. The buck moved from reach. Had Henry been with his usual hunting party the deer would have been dead long ago, but today he rode alone with only a simple weapon for company.

Angry, beaten by the charges of adultery and deceit against his beloved 'rose,' he rode off, ordering the others to leave him alone, on pain of death. Nobody doubted that the King would make good on his word should they follow.

The deer snorted and screamed, and Henry returned the call, his breath heavy and his leg aching. Too fat to turn quickly in his saddle he felt the buck pierce his leg from behind with its heavy antler. Henry wobbled and the horse lifted his front legs and then threw his back legs at the charging animal. The spear fell from Henry's grasp and landed on the deer's antlers.

The buck ran, but at the edge of the wood it paused; knees weakened, the spear landed with a crash at his hoofs. Henry dismounted and moved toward the injured animal, his own legs betraying him.

The King moved slowly, his breath made more noise than his feet on the dried leaves. The deer panted as the blood rushed faster from the wound. Henry's eyes never wavered as he came closer and held out his hand as though to offer some food in a gesture of forgiveness.

The buck's hardened eyes glanced away only once, to indicate the spear at its feet, as if to say, 'Come and get it.' They were ten paces away from one another now. Henry's leg throbbed, but he steeled himself against it. There was no show of weakness on the face of either creature as they waited for the other to drop to its knees and give way.

"I am the King of England," Henry said suddenly. "Fall to your knees at my name."

The buck's knees wobbled but did not break.

"I command you to die!" Henry raised his fist, but the deer snorted and shook its head. "Have you no idea that you are slashed and at death's door?"

Suddenly the buck moved. One step closer, two steps he came. Then three. He was an arm's length from the King now. His eyes looked upward into the King's face as his knees, at last, gave way. He fell with a thud at Henry's feet. The eyes remained open, softer.

The King could not turn away. He stared into the deer's eyes and lowered himself onto the ground next to him. He reached out his hand and stroked an antler.

"You too, were once a proud beast. Like me. My crown was once like yours, held magnificently upward toward the sky. Inspiring awe in all who saw it. And now, like you, I am old and weary and weak. Slain by love. Wounded in the heart. Laid bleeding to die. And who cares about me? No one. Just as no one cares for you. We are alone, you and I."

With a shudder, the buck died, and Henry lay his head upon the ground next to him.

The Tower was overcrowded. The Duchess was being held there, her mind filled with memories of the Countess of Salisbury and her messy beheading. It would do her no good to plead mercy on the grounds of her age. Joining her in the Tower were her step-children, the Countess of Bridgewater, Lord William Howard and his wife, Henry Howard, their children, and anybody else who might have known at some point that Katheryn had given her body to another.

Some of the prisoners were lucky. The Tower had become so overcrowded that the Royal Apartments were being used as well. The House of Howard had fallen and the Protestants were rejoicing. There was only one small deterrent to their happiness. The Duke of Norfolk, the most powerful of all the Howards, was still free. "I am prostrate at the King's feet" he declared in a letter to His Majesty. "The abominable deeds committed by the others in my family are no reflection on me. I join the King in condemning them." And then he disappeared for awhile to be certain he was out of harms way.

Culpeper's body was weak, but he managed to stand upright upon the gallows. He knew that he was to suffer merely a beheading and he said a silent prayer that the King saw fit to commute his sentence to the less painful one. Quietly he said to God, "I am guilty of the charge of desiring the Queen. But I swear to you, my heart became full with her, and although it was a crime I committed, I was helpless to do otherwise. I ask for your forgiveness." Publicly he spoke the words, "Pray for me, kind people." He knelt and with a single stroke his head was removed from his shoulders.

Francis witnessed this through eyes fogged by pain and fear. Not a nobleman like Culpeper, he was to die the full death. He had witnessed others die in the same manner. He knew what awaited him. Culpeper died with his clothes on; Francis would die stripped naked. He thought of the castration that would follow the hanging, and precede the disemboweling, and he wondered if he would be conscious enough to feel it.

"Strike off my head first, please," he whispered to the executioner.

"I cannot."

He stood, noose about his neck, wanting to speak a last word. To die nobly, without fear, chin held high. His throat was dry and his tongue stuck to the roof of his mouth. He managed to nod to the crowd before the noose tightened and choked his airway. He felt his eyeballs push their way out of the sockets and he fainted away. Only the sharp pain of the knife slicing his flesh revived him momentarily before he disappeared forever.

Katheryn screamed when she heard that Culpeper and Derehem had been killed. She recalled the time in Tyburn she witnessed the death of the priests and she couldn't bear the image that wouldn't release her. Derehem and Culpeper side-by-side, naked, their beautiful bodies marked by torture and their faces purple with suffocation. Worse was what would greet them after they were cut down.

"Thomas was spared the full execution," whispered her servant. "Francis was not. He was hanged, dismembered, bowelled, beheaded and quartered." She bowed and moved from the room leaving Katheryn with this new image to fill her senses and send her into hysteria.

There was a madness in Katheryn now. She could no longer harbor thoughts that the King would pardon her, call her his 'rose without a thorn' and take her back; or even divorce her as he had done with Anna of Cleves. The image of her cousin, Anne Boleyn dying by the sword had haunted Katheryn since she was a young lady and now it was her destiny as well.

"A sword. I must have a sword as Anne did. She died well they say. I will die in the same manner. Beautiful and proud, a French swordsman shall be my executioner."

She glanced from her window to see a wet snow, mixed with sleet, fall heavily upon the ground. "It will soon be Christmas. I wonder if the King is merry, celebrating the season with joy." She reached out the window to feel the cold wetness upon her fingers. "I am sure to rot in Hell for my crimes, but be certain, dear King that you shall join me there. I hope you choke on a bone, you fat evil monster."

This struck her as quite humorous and she laughed loudly. "We shall all be there! The entire Tudor court shall take up residence in Hell. All except the pious Miss Jane Seymour. She shall laugh at us from heaven."

She paused as she remembered a piece of history. "It was you he killed my cousin Anne for. Do not forget that you pious, evil witch. You are not so innocent. You probably laughed with the King when you heard of Anne's death and together you celebrated the overthrow of the Great Whore. And you, Catherine of Aragon, were you as pure as they say? Have you no secrets hidden in your closet? Oh, I suspect we shall all be in hell together. And Cromwell and Henry and Wolsey and even the Duchess shall meet her end as the Lady Salisbury did. And leading us all into the darkest reaches of the underworld shall be my uncle the Duke of Norfolk. We are doomed, all of us!"

She started a laugh that would not stop and skipped about the room yelling, "See you in Hell, you bloody bastards! See you in Hell!"

# CHAPTER 27

January 29th found the King in better humor. He entered the room puffed-up and eager to show the world that he was not the defeated man he was rumored to be. Those who were seated rose to attention; those who were standing bowed. He circled the hushed room like a general reviewing his troops—nodding his approval and speaking the occasional word of encouragement. The atmosphere was not calm tonight but buzzed with the unspoken knowledge that the Queen was soon to be executed. All knew it—the only question was when and how? It hung ominously over the ensemble. Only the King seemed unaware of the tension. He paused at every beautiful woman and when a lady pleased his eye he gave her a nod and bestowed his royal attention on her. It occurred to more than a few in attendance that already the King was looking for wife number six.

He took his place at the table and announced, "I am feeling strong. I ride and hunt daily. Take a good look at your King. He is still a man to be reckoned with."

With that he plopped down into his chair and with a wave of his hand ordered the others to do likewise. When he lifted a cup to his mouth it was a signal to relax and enjoy the evening. Soon the courtier's chatter filled the room and the ensemble was almost able to convince themselves that it was perfectly normal for the King to no longer be with his young bride. Although she was on their minds, nobody dared mention her name.

Sixty-one ladies attended the banquet he was hosting and he scanned the room hoping to find one to destroy the lingering memory of his imprisoned wife. He leaned over to the Duke of Suffolk, seated next to him, and gave him a wink. "See the lady at the far end of the table?" He pointed to a brown-haired beauty flirting with the man next to her.

"Yes, Your Majesty. I believe I know the lady of whom you speak." The Duke of Suffolk shook his head. He couldn't believe that Henry had forgotten the impending death of this last wife with such apparent ease. "It is the estranged wife of the poet Thomas Wyatt." He paused to see if the full ramification of his selection would sink in. The King looked at him blankly.

"Remember? The poet. You sent him to the Tower. He was in love with Anne Boleyn, I believe, before you married her." He didn't mention the fact that it was Katheryn Howard who was responsible for getting him released.

Henry did not flinch at the mention of Anne's name but merely said, "Then he has a good eye for the ladies, that poet. But what else are poets good for if not to make the rest of us aware of the beauty that surrounds us? And how are they to accomplish that task if they too have an ordinary eye?"

"Good point, Your Majesty." The Duke of Suffolk took a large sip of wine. He feared the next question, and only had to wait a moment until he heard it.

"Introduce her to me. Send her over here and place a chair beside me. I should like to have a word with her." The King nodded his head and gave the Duke a shove. "Go on, do as I say."

The Duke rose from his chair and when he was about half-way to reaching her, he noticed her dinner conversation had ceased and a look of unease had crossed her face. She stared at him and swallowed.

"Elizabeth Brooke, I believe," said the Duke of Suffolk. She smiled and nodded her head in agreement. "The King wishes you to be seated next to him. He requests your company for the remainder of the evening."

She turned to her companion and smiled. "Excuse me," was all she said before offering her hand to the Duke.

Her walk to the King's side brought the attention of the entire room upon her. She was composed and did not acknowledge the gazes.

She bowed when she neared him and said, "It was gracious of Your Majesty to request my company. I hope I do not disappoint."

"You will not. I'm certain of it." He motioned for her to be seated, and she did so, then waited to see what was expected of her.

"They tell me you are the estranged wife of the poet Thomas Wyatt. He has left you alone, I see."

"Perhaps, Your Majesty has forgotten. It was a condition of his release from the Tower that he resume conjugal relations with me. We had been apart for fifteen years and Your Majesty felt it improper. Upon Thomas' release we have been reunited, however, I must say that even the King cannot force my husband to love me. Nor can you require that I feel anything but admiration for him. He is indeed a great poet, but has proven himself to be less accomplished as a husband. But then, my wifely duties have not been much to speak of."

The King stared at her. He was astonished by her forthrightness. "And where is this estranged husband of yours at this moment?"

"He felt it was safer to stay away from court."

"He is a wise man then," said Henry. "You are very beautiful."

"Thank you, Your Majesty." She lifted a glass of wine to her lips. Henry resumed eating. An awkward silence descended between them.

From across the room a whispered voice reached their ears. "That's Elizabeth Brooke. She's a notorious adulteress. As if the King needs another one of those!"

Henry turned his reddened face quickly toward the sound to catch the person who spoke the words. He could not find the offender and returned to his food, feeling suddenly very tired and old.

# CHAPTER 28

On Friday, February 10<sup>th</sup>, the door to Katheryn's bedchamber flew open. She lifted her head in horror as the Duke of Suffolk and a dozen soldiers burst in on her without warning. In a single motion the curtains were pushed aside. Curling her body like a tormented caterpillar she drew away.

"No!" she screamed over and over and dove to the floor. Head first, belly down, she scrambled under the bed, kicking her feet wildly at the two soldiers who leaned down to extract her roughly by grabbing each an ankle and dragging her like a frightened hare from its hole.

Her screams pierced the heart of the Duke of Suffolk, who softened momentarily at the sight of the Queen flailing her arms as the soldiers attempted to hold her. The act of restricting her arms sent the Queen into such hysterics that it appeared she might simply die from the struggle. He ordered them to release her. Immediately, she threw herself prostrate at his feet and clawed his legs, desperately demanding her innocence be recognized.

"My God! Help me! I have begged for forgiveness. Please sirs, have I not suffered enough? I beg of you, have mercy on me."

"Get off your knees!" said the Duke of Suffolk. He bent down and lifted her with one hand as she clutched his wrists and stared into his eyes with fierce madness. "You were the Queen of England! Die with dignity, not like the whore you are said to be!"

"Whore! How dare you call the Queen a whore!"

But it was no use, she was no longer Queen in the eyes of either the King or these men, and her order had no more power than that of a lice-ridden street urchin.

"Get dressed!" he said. "Where are your gentlewomen? Get them in here to assist you. We are taking you to the Tower, where you will await your sentence. Mourn your own death. For it is certain that the King will not."

A pale-faced, trembling servant girl entered the room and looked at Katheryn. She had been ordered to dress the Queen in black. Katheryn stood obediently as the garments were put on her body. She wept bitterly, spilling her tears upon the black velvet fabric and wiping her eyes and nose upon the sleeve. A black hood, lined, not with jewels as would have once befitted her rank as Queen of England, but trimmed merely in satin brocade, was pulled over her hair and hung low on her face covering her forehead. She stood frozen in the center of the cold room as the men burst in once again and surrounded her tiny body. Then with moans escaping from beneath the black hood, Katheryn Howard was taken to the covered barge that would transport her to the dreaded Tower.

She walked to the river's edge in a trance. The black skirt swished back and forth with each step, and she forced her mind to focus on simple things. The smell of the soldier on her right was sour and she wondered what he had eaten to cause such an odor. The drone of the Duke's voice at her back took her attention, as did the sniffle of her lady beside her. Would it rain today? Perhaps snow? My, it was cold. She forgot where she was until she stopped to lift her eyes and saw the boat. Immediately panic rose in her chest and forced itself out of her mouth as a gasp.

She felt the soldiers tighten their grip upon her upper arms. She pulled back away from the barge. "Please, no," she said. "Please! No!" She turned to run, but there was no where to go.

Her small barge was escorted by a larger one stuffed with the Duke of Suffolk and his soldiers. They made their way past the London Bridge. A damp, dreary fog covered much of the land today but was not dense enough to conceal a vicious sight. Upon the London Bridge, high above the huddled figure of Katheryn Howard, were the decapitated heads of the two greatest loves of her life. Francis Dereham and Thomas Culpeper sat on spikes, side-by-side, and witnessed with vacant eye sockets the procession of their once passionate, vibrant Queen as she made her way down the river toward death.

# CHAPTER 29

Katheryn was in the Tower. She awaited her death. There would be no trial, for the Act of Attainder was to be used against her, as it was against Cromwell and countless others. It had to receive the King's signature before the execution could be performed and the Council was eager to save Henry from further distress. Surely, they agreed, he had suffered enough. It was arranged for The Great Seal to be attached in lieu of the King's signature. So it was on Saturday, February 11th, the Act was read in Parliament to the assembled members and Henry's assent officially proclaimed by all those but the King. Katheryn was to die on Monday. On Sunday she requested the block to lay her head upon.

Monday, February 13, 1542 was cold, dull and frosty. It was seven in the morning and the King's Council, all except the Dukes of Norfolk and Suffolk, (they had chosen to be absent) came to Katheryn's room to begin the long walk to the Tower Green. Today, both Katheryn and her Lady Rochford would meet their end. A black cloth shrouded the scaffold. It had been strewn with straw to keep the ladies blood from running freely over the boards.

Katheryn felt the vital fluid cease in her veins, and she fainted from the weakness overwhelming her. I do not know how to die. Dear God, you must help me die. I do not know how to die. How do I do this? I do not know how, looped endlessly through her brain. She was unable to hold onto anything that might be of help to her. No experiences, no thoughts, no feelings could assist her in this task.

How do I place my head upon a block of wood, willingly, to have it cut off? Was it possible for a human being to lean over and lay her head down, knowing full well that an axe would descend and remove it? In what part of her body, mind or soul did this ability lie? She searched frantically to find it, but discovered only the thought—dear God, you have not prepared me for this.

Her limbs became so limp that she wondered for a moment if she were not dead already. She fell left, then right supported by the soldiers who assisted her. She was ringed by the entire Council and other ladies and gentlemen, but she was no longer aware of any of them.

They had disappeared into the fog that surrounded her mind and separated her from the world. She searched the fog for God, hoping that He would appear and remove her from all this by drawing her into Him before the axe fell.

She stood before the block of wood. The same one she spent the night with. She uttered disconnected words. These are not my words, she thought, even as they left her mouth. "…my offenses against God which I heinously committed from my youth upward in breaking all of His commandments, and also against the King's Royal Majesty very dangerously."

Uttering those words brought forth the thought: Love cannot be forced, and I was forced to marry the King against my will. All that time my heart cried out for love; to long for the one who longed for me. In those brief moments, she remembered her father's face. She loved him dearly and had seen him so little. She knew he meant well in sending her to live with the Duchess—yet she missed his company. Silently, she said goodbye—I love you, Papa. She thought of the stable-boy she had romped with as a child. And Henry Mannox. I love all of you, she thought. For without you, my life would have had little pleasure. My indiscretions were also my enjoyment, for we loved each other in those moments we shared. Silently, she thanked each and every one of the men she had known for giving her happiness.

She remembered how Francis and Thomas met their end and it gave her body strength. I will be noble as they most certainly were. She turned to the spectators and paused. She stared into the eyes of Archbishop Cranmer—those sad eyes, resigned to the world's pain. Her gaze broadened to include them all, but she returned once again to the Archbishop. Something in those eyes filled her with defiance and a sense of purpose.

In her last few moments on Earth, Katheryn proclaimed the truth of her heart and uttered a simple statement. "I die the Queen of England, but I would rather have died the wife of Thomas Culpeper."

The audience gasped. With that she knelt, and placed her head upon the block. Yes, she would do it all again—no other path was available to her.

Her blood ran in red rivers, before being soaked up by the straw. Her weeping ladies gathered up her remains in a black blanket and removed them for burial.

It was now Lady Rochford's turn. She knelt before the blood-soaked block; no one had thought that perhaps she might like a clean piece of wood upon which to place her neck.


Henry VIII stood alone and looked out his bedroom window at the bleak countryside surrounding Hampton Palace.

"Your Majesty?" His servant entered the room, cautiously. The King did not stir. "Your Majesty?"

The wind caught the door and slammed it shut with a bang.

Henry jumped.

"Your Majesty. It is done."

# *EPILOGUE*

## KATHERYN HOWARD

No one knows the actual date she was born—not even the year. She has been given many different dates of birth, but all of them are guesses. No one knows what she looked like. No authenticated portrait of her exists. There are only descriptions of her beauty and grace. Her name is spelled Katherine, Catherine, Kathryn and Katheryn—the one surviving letter from her to Thomas Culpeper is signed Katheryn. In many ways she is a mystery—she lived and died a Queen but was never coronated. In the 19<sup>th</sup> century there were reported sightings of her ghost racing down the hallway toward the chapel where Henry was praying after he'd had her locked in her room.

## HENRY VIII

In 1543, Henry VIII remarried for the sixth time; although after divorcing Anne of Cleves, and Katheryn's execution, it was difficult to find a woman eager to tie the knot. The fact that a maid who did not reveal her sexual liaisons prior to meeting the King could be killed, as Katheryn Howard had been, made marrying him a risky proposition. So, Henry settled on a widow of thirty-one, Katherine Parr. Although previously married, Katherine was childless and more than likely barren. After having spent his life replacing wives until he could get one to bear him son, he chose a woman with whom there was little chance of producing an heir.

Katherine Parr almost suffered the same fate as Katheryn Howard when the King objected to her strong opinions and disagreeing with him. Henry initiated plans to have her arrested, but word leaked out to her. Katherine rushed to

Henry's side and assured him that he had complete sovereignty over her. Henry forgave Katherine her previous "indiscretions," but did not inform the Lord Chancellor. Forty guards came to arrest Katherine, as they had been instructed. The King turned on them, blaming them entirely for the intrusion.

Henry VIII died on January 28, 1547. He was fifty-five years old and he reigned for nearly thirty-eight years. Katherine Parr outlived him.

## ANNE OF CLEVES

After the marriage dissolved, Anne was known by the title "King's Sister," and stayed on good terms with Henry. She was given Hever Castle, the former home of Anne Boleyn, and enough money to live quite well, provided she did not move overseas. She lived quietly in the countryside until 1557 and never remarried. She is buried in a tomb in Westminster Abbey.

## THE HOWARD CLAN

The entire Howard clan was rounded up and imprisoned—servants, important and minor members of the family. Even the Duchess of Norfolk was arrested and imprisoned. On December 22, 1541 the whole family (with the exception of the Duke) was found guilty of treason for concealing Katheryn's sexual offenses. They stood to lose all their property and to be imprisoned for life. Most were released within months but the Duchess remained imprisoned until May 1542—primarily for burning Derehem's papers.

## DUKE OF NORFOLK

After Katheryn's imprisonment Norfolk was not arrested for treason along with the rest of his family. Henry may have looked favorably on him, in part, due to a letter he wrote the King proclaiming his innocence. However, the tides turned against him in 1546 when he and his son, Henry Howard, earl of Surrey, were arrested for treason. His son was executed, but Norfolk managed to escape the same fate because of Henry's timely death. When Henry's daughter, Mary, took the throne she had Norfolk released from prison and restored his dukedom. Once again, Norfolk had influence in the court. In 1554 he successfully led his forces against the rebellion of Sir Thomas Wyatt, the younger.

## EDWARD VI

Henry's only son, Edward (produced by his third wife, Jane Seymour) reigned briefly from 1547-1553. He died at the age of fifteen after five and a half years of rule. During his brief reign the Protestants gained the upper hand in England. His youth provided a perfect backdrop for power plays in the court, especially between the Catholics and Protestants. In Henry's will it stated that Edward, then Mary, then Elizabeth should reign in that order, following his death. A brief power struggle ensued when an attempt was made to place Lady Jane Grey on the throne following Edward's death. It lasted for nine days until Henry's wishes were restored and Mary Tudor took her rightful place.

## MARY I

Henry VIII's daughter from his first marriage to Catherine of Aragon, Mary Tudor, was born in 1516 and took the throne in 1553. She reigned until 1558. She was a staunch Catholic. She married Philip II of Spain, but was did not produce a child. Her first act was to appeal the Protestant legislation of her brother, Edward VI. She was responsible for burning almost 300 people at the stake for their Protestant beliefs—including Archbishop Cranmer. This earned her the nickname, "Bloody Mary."

## ARCHBISHOP CRANMER

Archbishop Cranmer's life ended when Mary Tudor had him arrested for his Protestant beliefs. At 67, Cranmer, tired of imprisonment, recanted his faith. What he didn't know was that it didn't matter—they planned to burn him anyway. Before he was to be burned, he once again proclaimed his belief in the Protestant faith.

0-595-31301-9

Printed in the United States
42460LVS00003B/138